"I'm going to have to soak in a hot tub for an hour just to get all this grime off me," Roxie said with a laugh.

Tyler almost groaned out loud at the thought of her sitting naked in his antique bathtub, water glistening on her rosy skin. . . . He had to stop thinking this way about her!

"I have to go now," he said abruptly, and headed down the stairs for the door.

"What's wrong, Tyler?" Roxie called just as he was halfway there.

He laughed, but it wasn't a happy sound. "What's wrong?" he said in disbelief. Didn't she realize how she tempted him, even in his dreams? His eyes flashed, but he couldn't seem to pry his gaze from the wisp of lace that peered out from the deep collar of her blouse, just enough to tantalize and make him want to see more.

"You want to know what's wrong?" He retraced his steps, pulled her inside the apartment, and took her in his arms. Roxie stiffened in surprise, but in a moment she felt her resistance slip away, and she was warm and pliant in his arms. He kissed her deeply, urgently, whispering her name. "This is what's wrong, Red," he confessed. And, he wanted to add, what's right. . . .

WHAT ARE *LOVESWEPT* ROMANCES?

They are stories of true romance and touching emotion. We believe those two very important ingredients are constants in our highly sensual and very believable stories in the *LOVESWEPT* line. Our goal is to give you, the reader, stories of consistently high quality that may sometimes make you laugh, sometimes make you cry, but are always fresh and creative and contain many delightful surprises within their pages.

Most romance fans read an enormous number of books. Those they truly love, they keep. Others may be traded with friends and soon forgotten. We hope that each *LOVESWEPT* romance will be a treasure—a "keeper." We will always try to publish

LOVE STORIES YOU'LL NEVER FORGET
BY AUTHORS YOU'LL ALWAYS REMEMBER

The Editors

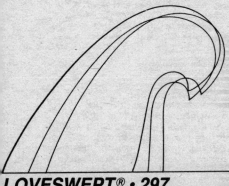

LOVESWEPT® • 297

Charlotte Hughes
Sweet Misery

BANTAM BOOKS
TORONTO • NEW YORK • LONDON • SYDNEY • AUCKLAND

SWEET MISERY

A Bantam Book / December 1988

LOVESWEPT® *and the wave device are registered*
trademarks of Bantam Books, a division of
Bantam Doubleday Dell Publishing Group, Inc.
Registered in U.S. Patent
and Trademark Office and elsewhere.

If you would be interested in receiving protective vinyl
covers for your Loveswept books, please write to this address
for information:

Loveswept
Bantam Books
P.O. Box 985
Hicksville, NY 11802

ISBN 0-553-21927-8

Published simultaneously in the United States and Canada

Bantam Books are published by Bantam Books, a division
of Bantam Doubleday Dell Publishing Group, Inc. Its trade-
mark, consisting of the words "Bantam Books" and the
portrayal of a rooster, is Registered in U.S. Patent and
Trademark Office and in other countries. Marca Registrada.
Bantam Books, 666 Fifth Avenue, New York, New York 10103.

PRINTED IN THE UNITED STATES OF AMERICA

O   0 9 8 7 6 5 4 3 2 1

To Mother with love.
You can't appreciate the sunshine
until first you've survived the storm

Prologue

March 3, 1968

Dear Reverend Norris:

I would like to thank you for your help. If it wasn't for you, I would still be sitting in that detention home with the rest of my friends for stealing. I deeply appreciate your taking me into your own home until you could find a place for me.

Mr. Lewis, the man you sent me to live with here in Charleston, is very kind and treats me like a son. He is teaching me the restaurant business and says I've learned more in six months than he has in thirty years. I hope to have my own restaurant one day.

I heard my parents left town. I don't think I'll ever remember them without seeing a bottle of whiskey in their hands.

Once again, thanks for your help. Give your daughter Roxie a big bear hug for me. For a five-year-old, she's a feisty little thing.

Remember, if I can ever return the favor, call me.

Sincerely,
Tyler Sheridan

May 5, 1988

Dear Tyler:

I hardly can believe the past twenty years have slipped by so quickly. You're no longer a troubled boy of thirteen; you're a man now.

Your restaurant has quite a reputation. Even in Summerville people are talking about it. You've done very well for yourself, but then I always knew you would, even way back when you were stealing hubcaps off automobiles.

I'm writing for a favor. Remember Roxie? She was five years old when you last saw her, I believe. Well she's a young woman of twenty-five now, but just as stubborn as she was as a youngster. She has decided to leave her teaching position here in Summerville and teach business management at a university in Charleston. As dean of our fine Baptist college, I'd hoped Roxie would stay on and build her life here as her brothers and sisters have done, but she claims she needs space, despite the fact she has had her own apartment for several years now.

What I'm asking on my daughter's behalf is that you give her a job if you have an opening. Since her teaching job doesn't start till fall, she'll need to support herself until then. She refuses to take a dime from me. I have asked Roxie to look you up the minute she hits town, just to say hello, which should be in about a month from now when school closes for the summer. With her working for you, I'll feel much better knowing there's someone to sort of keep an eye on her. I know I'm overprotective, but I still think of Roxie as my baby.

For the time being, why don't we let this be our little secret. If Roxie knew I'd come to you for help, she'd have a fit. She's one independent lady, for sure.

God bless you,
Rev. Franklin Norris

May 9, 1988

Dear Reverend Norris:

I genuinely am touched that you came to me for help. Your daughter will be in good hands, I assure you. Thank you for letting me return an old favor.

Sincerely,
Tyler Sheridan

One

Hellfire and damnation, she was lost again!

Roxie Norris screeched her old Plymouth to a halt to keep from running a red light and jerked the map from the seat beside her. After driving for six hours in a car with a broken air conditioner as the early, but very hot June sun blazed down on the metal roof, she was in no mood to spend the rest of the afternoon scouring the streets of Charleston in search of a man she hadn't laid eyes on since she was a little girl in pinafores. Her annoyance was clear in the vertical lines between her green eyes. A horn sounded from behind, telling her the light had changed. Roxie tossed the map aside and stepped on the gas.

Why was she hunting for a man named Tyler Sheridan? Because her father had insisted, that's why. "Be sure to look up my good friend Tyler the moment you arrive in Charleston," he'd told her. He had refused to let her go until he'd elicited a promise from her that she would. "He'll know what section of town you should consider when looking for an apartment," she could hear her father say. Roxie had passed at least a dozen nice-looking apartment complexes since she'd reached town. She hadn't come *close* to finding the Battery —the exclusive stretch of road where Sheridan's restaurant supposedly was located.

"Probably owns a hot dog stand," she muttered to herself.

The yacht club! she thought, as she drove past. Hadn't she seen that on the map? Yes, she finally was going in the right direction. The harbor winked at her in the sunshine, reflecting the sun's rays like a beveled mirror. The enormous mansions coming into sight filled her with awe.

Roxie was so caught up with taking in the sights, she almost missed the sign bearing the name Southern Belle Supper Club. She slammed on her brakes and turned her steering wheel sharply. Her car skidded between the lofty wrought-iron gates separating the grounds from the street.

For a moment all she could do was stare ahead as her car sputtered up the hill toward a pristine white mansion. A navy blue awning marked the entrance. This was no hot dog stand; her father's friend was obviously rich, she decided.

Roxie suddenly felt self-conscious in her crumpled yellow dress. Her white Peter Pan collar, which had been clean and crisp that morning, hung limply around her throat. Her long red hair, which she'd gathered into a ponytail, made her look eighteen instead of twenty-five.

Well, ol' moneybags was just going to have to accept her as she was!

The lawn surrounding the mansion was perfectly manicured and embellished with flowering trees and shrubs. Tall magnolias with fat white blossoms sweetened the air. Camellia bushes in a blaze of color lined the winding drive. Bright pink flowers lay scattered like colorful snowflakes around sprawling mimosas. Even the crepe myrtle was in full bloom, she noted, their fragile limbs pruned and the bark bleached white from the sun.

The scenery had so captivated Roxie's attention, that before she knew it she found herself sitting right beneath the impressive awning. This would not do, she told herself. The best place for her car was in the back row of the parking lot, out of sight. She wasn't about to let her father's rich friend see the wreck she was driving. Quickly she stepped on the gas. Much to her surprise the car lurched forward, then refused to budge.

For a moment Roxie sat in stunned silence. "Stupid car," she muttered, and jerked the gear shift into neutral. Again and again she shifted gears. Her last attempt was met with a high-pitched whine.

Roxie glanced around anxiously. Perhaps she could find a gas station nearby and have the car towed away before anyone noticed. Yes, that's what she'd do. She opened the door and climbed out of the car. With her purse slung over one shoulder, she hurried down the hill.

Roxie made her way down the sidewalk at a trot, trying to ignore the strange looks she received from passersby. When she heard a car slow beside her, she glanced up and found herself looking into the sweet faces of two elderly ladies. The car came to a stop, and one of the ladies motioned Roxie over.

"Is something wrong, dearie?" the woman on the passenger side asked, the lines around her mouth etched in concern.

Roxie hurried over to the car and, between gulps of air, tried to explain her situation. "So you see, I really need to get to a gas station fast," she said.

"Get in the car, honey," the driver said, her voice as sweet as her smile. "We'll take you wherever you need to go."

"I really appreciate this," Roxie said, climbing into the back seat. The driver, who had a cap of snowy white hair, introduced herself as Ellie.

"And I'm Dorothy," the other woman said, turning her silver head in Roxie's direction. Roxie told them her name and settled herself comfortably in the back seat, thankful she'd run into the two ladies. They reminded her of the ladies who sang in her father's church choir. She chatted easily with them.

"What do you think is wrong with your car?" Ellie asked once they got acquainted.

Roxie moaned. "I have no idea. I've replaced

almost everything under the hood. Except the transmission."

"A new transmission could cost as much as four hundred dollars," Ellie pointed out.

Roxie nodded solemnly. "I know. And I only have eight hundred dollars to my name. I was planning to open a checking account this afternoon, then look for an apartment. Just a studio," she added. "Something inexpensive."

"Here we are, dear," Ellie said, pulling into a gas station. "You run in and see if you can get somebody to tow your car. We'll wait for you." She shook her head when Roxie reached for her purse. "I wouldn't carry that in there if I were you," she warned. "Not if you've got a lot of cash in your wallet."

"Ellie's right," Dorothy said, glancing at their surroundings skeptically.

Roxie nodded. "Of course. I keep forgetting I'm in a big city now." She dropped her purse onto the seat. "I'll try to hurry." The women gave her smiles as sweet as Karo syrup as she closed the door.

Roxie hurried into the gas station, where a man sat with both feet propped on a desk. "Do you have a tow truck?" she asked politely. When he said he did, she explained her situation.

"My boy, Leroy, can tow it in for you. It'll cost you twenty-five dollars."

"Fine. Can he do it right away?"

"If you've got the money, he's got the time."

"Okay, let me tell my friends, then," she said, backing toward the door.

The man glanced through the window behind her and frowned. "Looks like your friends decided not to wait," he said, pointing toward the gas pumps. "They just tossed something into the trash can and drove off."

Roxie swung her head around. Sure enough, the car had disappeared. She ran out the door, her eyes scanning the streets. There was no sign of Ellie and Dorothy's car anywhere. She checked the garbage can and found her purse dumped in among some wet paper towels. Her heart sank. She retrieved her purse immediately, already dreading what she would find. Her wallet was empty.

"What happened?" the man said, coming up to stand beside her.

Roxie's mouth formed a grim line. "I've been robbed by the Medicare Mob."

Roxie hung up the receiver of the pay telephone and leaned her head against it. The owner of the gas station had resumed his position at the desk, while his son clattered around in the garage. "I'm going to have to go to the police station personally to file a report," she said, heaving an enormous sigh. "Not that I can tell them a whole lot. I didn't get the car's license number. I don't know where the ladies live, nor did they tell me their last names."

"Smart crooks," the man said. "Now, about towing your car in—"

"I can pay for it," Roxie said quickly, still unable to believe the women had robbed her deliberately. "I have fifty dollars in one of my suitcases locked in the trunk of my car. I sewed it into the lining in case of an emergency, and I think this definitely qualifies as one. Let's go."

Roxie arrived back at the Southern Belle twenty minutes later in a tow truck driven by a bashful, tongue-tied Leroy. She was so distraught over having her money stolen, she almost missed seeing a tow truck heading in the opposite direction with her car attached. "Stop!" she told Leroy. "There goes my car!"

Leroy skidded to a halt as Roxie pried the door open. "Watch your step," he warned, a split second too late.

Roxie missed the step altogether. When she landed hard on the concrete drive, her right heel jammed into a hole. She sprang forward as pain sliced through her foot and ankle. She grasped the side window of the truck to keep from falling on her face. For a moment the spasms ricocheting through her foot and ankle had her undivided attention. The tow truck bearing her car passed her by. She tried to lift her foot and winced as more pain shot through the ankle. Her heel was stuck in a hole. She very carefully lifted her foot from the shoe, hanging onto the door handle and balancing herself precariously on her good foot. She yanked at the shoe, and after several attempts it popped out, minus the heel. "My best pumps," she said aloud, remembering she'd spent almost thirty-five dollars for them.

Suddenly all her anger and frustration surfaced. "Dammit!" she said, and threw the shoe as hard as she could at a mimosa bush. Bright pink petals fluttered to the ground like fat raindrops, but she didn't notice. Her problems seemed insurmountable. She had no job, no place to live, and no transportation. Not to mention the fact that a tow truck had just driven away with her luggage and her last fifty bucks.

"Damn, damn, damn!" she muttered angrily, and stamped her foot against the asphalt drive. She bowed her head as tears sprang to her eyes from the excruciating pain. Then she saw a large, booted foot, and her eyes widened in surprise.

Her gaze inched upward, taking in a pair of denims so faded, they had a white sheen to them. Tightly encased in the worn fabric were a pair of lean but slightly muscular thighs. Her gaze crawled past a western-style belt and a grease-stained T-shirt that strained over the broadest shoulders she'd ever laid eyes on. Then, suddenly, she found herself looking into a pair of warm brown eyes. His face was rough, bronzed from the sun, but he was devastatingly handsome. The corners of his eyes and mouth were turned upward slightly, as though he found something funny.

"Are you having a fit or what?" he asked, gazing at her steadily.

His mocking words and cocky stance set her on edge and fanned the heat of her anger. She glared at him. "Are you responsible for having my car towed away?" she asked, examining his attire once again with a critical eye. He's probably the cook, she thought, and a heathen as well. No decent man would wear pants that tight. And only the devil himself would have a mouth as sexy and hair as black as midnight.

He crossed his arms over his chest, his gaze devouring the slender woman with the flaming red hair and vibrant green eyes. "You call that thing a car?" he said in a drawl that made the back of her throat itch. "Looked like the only thing holding it together was rust and mud."

Well, of all the nerve! she thought. She certainly wasn't dealing with a gentleman. Where she came from, men wore neat slacks and crisp white dress shirts. This man was almost crude the way his pants molded to his . . . person.

"And what do you drive, Calvin Klein," she remarked, "a Mercedes-Benz?"

The smile he gave her was lazy but brazen as hell. "As a matter of fact—"

"I'd like to speak to Mr. Sheridan," she said, cutting him off. "I am going to report you."

"Report me?"

Roxie heard snickering and for the first time noticed several men in the background. She inched her chin higher. "That's right," she said, turning her attention back to him. "You had no right to have my car towed away, and I intend to see that I'm reimbursed."

"And you had no right leaving it parked in front of the doorway."

She almost choked on her anger. Who was he, the doorman, for heaven's sake? she wondered. "Well, it just so happens I was trying to get a tow truck here as fast as I could to move it. Little did I know I would be robbed of all my money—except for the small amount I'd left in my luggage in the trunk of my car, which *you* had towed off!" She had to stop to catch her breath.

"You were robbed?" he asked in surprise.

"Not that it's any of your business, but yes. And when I tell Mr. Sheridan what you've put me through . . ." She huffed. "It just so happens I know him personally," she added in what she hoped was her most menacing voice. She'd do anything to wipe that smirk off his face. He obviously thought he was someone special.

"You don't say," he said, strolling casually toward the mimosa bush. He reached for her shoe and saw that her heel was missing. He carried it over and handed it to her. "Have you got something against bushes?"

She decided it was best to ignore the man. She stepped into the shoe cautiously. It looked silly without the heel, but she wouldn't give him the satisfaction of showing her embarrassment.

He planted his hands on his hips and cocked his head to the side, studying her face closely for a minute. "Lady, I think I would remember if we had met before. Not only because of that nasty temper of yours, but I don't believe I've ever seen hair that color." Or legs so shapely, he thought to himself.

"I refuse to discuss anything further with you," she said. "I'll find Mr. Sheridan myself."

The man stepped in front of her. She glanced up reluctantly.

"You're looking at him, Red."

Two

Roxie almost reeled at the words. "You!" The word was expelled on a gasp and sounded like an accusation. "You're Tyler Sheridan? The . . . uh . . . owner?" When he merely nodded, her eyes widened in disbelief. "But you don't look like . . . I mean . . ." He certainly didn't dress the part, and she had expected someone older. This man looked to be in his early thirties—much too young, in her opinion, to own such a fine place.

"You'll have to excuse the way I'm dressed," he said, as though reading her thoughts. "I was cleaning the grill. Now would you mind telling me who *you* are, and why you were throwing a temper tantrum in my driveway? For a minute I thought I was going to have to shoot you to put you out of your misery."

Roxie summoned all the saints in heaven to

force a great earthquake to suddenly split the ground and swallow her. A hot blush crept up her neck and face, and she was certain that if a person literally could die of humiliation, she'd be a goner. Perhaps she should lie and spare her father the embarrassment of claiming to be his daughter, she thought.

"Well?" There was a look of expectancy on the man's handsome face.

She mumbled her name, and he cupped the back of one ear with the palm of his hand to show he hadn't heard her. "I said I'm . . . uh . . . Roxanne Norris," she confessed a bit louder, and saw his brows draw together in a frown. "Roxie to my friends," she added. "I believe you know my father, Reverend Franklin Norris."

Tyler's face went blank. "*You're* Reverend Norris's little girl?" He didn't notice the look of irritation his comment evoked. "Boy, have you grown up!" He smiled. "So has your temper."

Roxie's blush deepened. "I never claimed to be perfect."

His gaze traveled over the length of her body. He was still unable to believe the change in her. "What happened to your ankle?" he asked, noticing the swelling for the first time.

Roxie glanced down at her ankle, surprised to see it was twice its original size. "I think I twisted it," she said. "I caught the heel of my shoe in a crack in the concrete when I climbed out of the truck." She waved the matter aside as though it held no importance. Right now all she wanted to do was find her car and disappear. Her stomach churned with anxiety, and her chest felt as if it might burst. She knew her feelings had very little to do with the mishaps that had befallen her so far. She blamed the man's compelling brown eyes, the confident set of his shoulders, and the raw masculinity he exuded. Her father had not prepared her for the likes of Tyler Sheridan.

"I'm really sorry about that," he said, his thick brows bunched together in concern. "I'm having the drive repaved next week." He tried to keep his gaze focused on her ankle instead of on her legs, which were long and silky looking and made him think of hosiery commercials. He could almost envision them folded across a man's back—*his* back—and crossed tightly at the ankles. No doubt her thighs were equally nice and . . . aw damn, what was he thinking? She was his old friend's daughter, not some dancer in a nightclub he had paid money to leer at. He cleared his throat, but his voice was gruff when he spoke.

"It's getting red and puffy. Does it hurt?"

"It's not as bad as it looks," she said, trying to convince herself as much as him. She was anxious to shift the conversation from her to her car. She was still trying to figure out how she was going to pay the towing fee. "Now, about my car—"

"I'll take care of your car," he said quickly. "Hold on a second." He hurried over to the tow truck where Leroy sat cleaning his fingernails with a pocket knife as though he had all the time in the world. "The lady won't be needing you after all," he told the young man, slipping a twenty-dollar bill into his hand as he shook it.

The exchange went unnoticed by Roxie. She was studying her ankle and wondering just how much damage she'd done to it.

"I'm going to have a doctor take a look at that ankle," Tyler said, watching as Leroy drove off.

Roxie tested the ankle again, gritting her teeth to keep from moaning. Of all times for something like this to happen, she thought. All she wanted to do was find a cheap motel room, soak her foot, and consider her options. Her circumstances had changed dramatically in the past hour, and she needed time to digest her predicament. Of course, she wasn't going to be able to afford *any* kind of motel room until she got her hands on the secret stash of money in her suitcase. Not that fifty dollars would get her very far, she realized.

"I appreciate your concern, Mr. Sheridan—"

"Tyler."

"And I wish we hadn't met under these circumstances. But what I'd really like to do is just get my car back and . . ." Get her car back and what? she asked herself. The blasted thing didn't run. Still, she'd feel better with it parked behind some garage or gas station until she could scrape up the money to have it repaired.

"Why don't we go inside and discuss it?" Tyler suggested. When she looked as though she might argue, he shrugged. "I don't see that you have much choice, Roxie. I *can* call you Roxie?" She nodded, and he went on. "You said someone robbed you. How much did they get?"

"Everything," she said dully. "Except the fifty dollars in my suitcase."

"Were you hurt?" he asked, wondering why he hadn't thought to check before. When she merely shook her head, he continued. "Do you think you could give the police an accurate description of the men who robbed you?"

"They were women," she said, then blushed when she saw the look of surprise on his face. "Big women," she added. "It was two against one."

The poor girl was really having a tough time of it, he realized. He owed it to her father to see that she got help. "Well, I'll have to call the police department to find out where your car is. I'll have someone come down and take your report."

"I've already called the police," she said, "but there was nothing I could tell them. I don't know who the ladies were or where they lived." She had suffered enough humiliation today. She wasn't about to tell him the robbers were snowy-haired elderly ladies. And she'd rather die than confess her naïveté in leaving her purse in a car with two perfect strangers. She probably had the word "hick" written all over her face.

"Let's finish this discussion inside," he said, "and get out of the sun. I want to put an ice pack on that ankle. And stop looking so worried. We'll get all this worked out," he told her.

All her defenses seemed to drift into thin air like wispy smoke rings from a fat cigar. Although his smile was disarming and sent her pulse racing, her own smile was forced. She was in a jam and she knew it. What bothered her more, though, was that he knew it. She hated feeling so helpless. She almost preferred calling her father for money to flashing her financial problems in front of this man like a neon sign.

"If you're worrying about the towing fine, don't," he said. "I had your car towed away and I will pay whatever is necessary to get it back. Now, come on inside and let's have a glass of iced tea."

"Thank you," she said stiffly, her way of acquiescing to his having paid the towing expenses. After all, he *was* responsible for having it towed away, why shouldn't he pay for it? she decided.

"You're welcome." He made a production of offering his arm, and she hobbled toward him, giving him a weak smile. His own smile turned into a frown. "This isn't going to work," he said, shaking his head as he glanced down at her swollen ankle. Without another word, he leaned forward and swooped her off the ground and into his arms, turning a deaf ear to her protests. "Don't be ridiculous," he said, when she kept insisting she could walk. "You'll only injure yourself further."

"I'm too heavy," she said, thankful the group of men she'd noticed earlier had disappeared.

"Yeah, you must weigh at least one hundred and ten," he said, giving an exaggerated grunt. "You always were too skinny for your own good." Actually she felt pretty good—nice and soft and very feminine against him. She certainly had filled out in all the right places, he noted.

If Roxie had been uncomfortable before, she

was doubly so now, pressed against Tyler's broad chest. What was she supposed to do with her hands, for heaven's sake? She clutched her purse tightly. She might be able to avoid looking at him, but there was no way she could avoid *feeling* him or smelling his tangy after-shave. His biceps were hard and muscular, his stride powerful. She could feel the crisp hair on his arms rubbing the back of her thighs as he walked, chafing her pantyhose in a way that made her distressingly warm low in her belly.

"You still don't have that problem with your nose, do you?" he asked, gazing down at her face. Her skin was almost translucent and could have passed as fine porcelain had it not been for the smattering of freckles across her nose. When she gave him a blank look, he chuckled, and the deep rumbling sound in his chest made her toes curl. "You know, it used to run all the time. Whenever I thought of you, I thought of skinny legs, tangled red hair, and a runny nose."

"What an endearing image," she muttered. "I think my nose stopped running in second or third grade. It was allergies, I believe." Darn, why did he have to look at her so intensely? And why did his face have to be so close? She caught the scent of sweat and after-shave, and the very maleness of it made her insides as soft as warm taffy. Had she been a snail, she would have crawled into her shell long ago. She was thankful when they reached the front door, but instead of putting her down, Tyler merely shifted her in his arms so he could reach the brass doorknob.

A rush of cool air hit her when Tyler stepped into the foyer. Roxie was so overwhelmed with the grand entryway, she could only stare for a moment. A magnificent free-floating staircase dominated the room. She almost could envision Rhett Butler standing at the foot of the stairs waiting for his beloved Scarlett. "It's beautiful," she whispered, taking in the high ceilings and ornate crown molding and plasterwork.

Tyler smiled. "Glad you like it. You should have seen it before I had it restored. It was a shambles. One would have thought an entire Yankee infantry had passed through."

Roxie gazed at him thoughtfully as he carried her by an oak counter that supported an antique cash register. The counter was made of glass in front, revealing dozens of boxes of expensive cigars. She was beginning to wonder about the man in the grease-stained T-shirt. Not only was he obviously a hard worker and a smart businessman, she'd bet her last fifty dollars he was an incurable romantic as well. Who else would have gone to such trouble to see that the place was put back together precisely as it had been originally? The restoration alone probably cost more than the mansion itself, she guessed.

Tyler turned down a short hallway and carried her through an open door leading into an office that smelled of leather and pine. How appropriate, she thought, noticing the imposing mahogany desk and masculine furniture.

He set her gently on the leather couch, relieved

he was no longer holding her because her father had not prepared him for the grown-up version of his daughter. Tyler had expected a shy, scrawny country girl, not a redheaded she-devil with long, shapely legs and a body that begged to be caressed.

"Make yourself comfortable," Tyler said, "while I run to the kitchen and get some ice for your ankle." He closed the door behind him before she could respond.

Roxie decided it was useless to argue with him. He appeared to be a man who was accustomed to giving orders. Of course, that didn't mean she had to follow all of them, but for the time being, he seemed more able to make rational decisions. Her head was still spinning from all she'd been through since she'd hit town. And she had to admit she was exhausted—not to mention worried. Her ankle was looking worse by the minute. How was she ever going to look for a job with a sprained ankle? she wondered hopelessly.

Her musings were interrupted when someone tapped lightly on the door. A teenaged boy entered wearing a uniform and carrying a tray with two glasses of iced tea and some cheese and crackers. "Mr. Sheridan thought you might like some refreshment," he said, placing the tray carefully on the coffee table.

"Oh, I wish you hadn't gone to so much trouble," she said, feeling more burdensome by the moment. She thanked the boy, and he left. By the time Tyler arrived with a homemade ice pack, Roxie had finished her tea and was nibbling on a piece of cheese.

"You're going to have to lie down," Tyler said, reaching for several throw pillows. She did as he said, and he slipped one pillow beneath her head. Then he moved to her feet, where he elevated her bad ankle on two more cushions. "It's cold," he warned, before placing the ice pack gently on her bruised and swollen ankle. "By the way, I called a doctor. He should be here soon." When she started to object, he raised his hand to stop her. "Remember, you injured yourself on *my* property. It's my responsibility to see that you receive proper care." He caught her completely off guard by grinning. "It'll look good in court just in case you try to sue me."

So that was it, she thought. He was afraid of a lawsuit. "I'm not going to sue you," she said, gazing up at him. She couldn't help wondering if he were merely trying to make her feel less a hindrance.

Within an hour both the doctor and a police officer had arrived. The doctor examined her ankle, which he diagnosed as sprained. He wrapped it tightly and told her to stay off it for a few days. The officer, who waited patiently just outside the office, came in once the doctor had left and took down the facts of the robbery. Roxie was thankful Tyler had excused himself beforehand to check on the whereabouts of her car and to finish cleaning the grill so it would be ready by the time the restaurant opened at six.

As soon as Roxie signed the police report, the officer stood up to go, promising to notify her if he learned anything. Roxie was left alone in the impressive office once again. The room somewhat resembled a studio apartment, she thought. She hobbled to one door, opened it, and found an entire wardrobe of clothes. Another door led into a bathroom, complete with shower. Roxie bathed her face in cold water at the sink and dried it with a towel that smelled of Tyler's after-shave. She turned a critical eye toward the sofa. She was certain it opened into a bed, and she wondered how many nights Tyler slept there—and with whom. The last thought surprised her as much as it embarrassed her. What business was it of hers who the man entertained? Not knowing what else to do with herself, Roxie lay back down on the couch, elevated her foot on the pillow, and closed her eyes. She wondered where Tyler was, and if he'd learned anything about her car. After a moment she drifted off to sleep.

"Roxie?"

"Hmmm?"

"Are you awake?"

Roxie's eyelids fluttered open, and she blinked several times in surprise when she found Tyler kneeling on one knee beside the couch. "I must've fallen asleep," she said apologetically.

"Which isn't surprising considering all you've been through," he said, reaching over to adjust the ice bag. "I'm afraid I have bad news." As she arched a pair of lovely brows in question, he grinned sheepishly. "The police lost your car."

"Lost it?" she said dumbly, trying to digest the information while her brain was still foggy from sleep.

"I'm afraid so. The police department has no record of having impounded it. They assured me it would turn up. I'm supposed to call them back tomorrow."

Suddenly, her eyes widened in horror. "Tomorrow? But what about my clothes? And my money?" What was she going to do now, for heaven's sake? She certainly didn't want to call her father. He'd wire her a bus ticket and insist she return home immediately. She'd be the laughingstock of Summerville. Poor little Roxie Norris, they'd say. She couldn't even make it on her own in the big city for one day. No, she'd rather die first. But what was her alternative?' She'd have to sleep on the streets. Oh, Lord, this was turning out to be a real-life version of *The Out-of-Towners*, she thought.

As though reading her thoughts, Tyler touched her hand gently. Oddly enough Roxie found his touch comforting, despite her bleak circumstances. "You're coming home with me, Roxie," he said matter-of-factly.

"What?" At first she assumed he was joking, but when she looked up, she found he was serious. "I can't stay at your place," she said. "I'll just have to make other arrangements." She'd sleep in a bus station first. Tyler Sheridan's mere presence made her so edgy she couldn't think straight.

"Look, if you're worrying about what your father will say, don't. I'll call him and explain the situation. Besides, we'll be well chaperoned. I have a housekeeper who's twice my size. In fact, she could probably whip me with one hand tied behind her back."

Roxie knew he was trying to put her at ease with his teasing remarks, but it didn't work. "Why should you call my father?" she said coolly. "I'm twenty-five years old. I certainly don't need his permission." She wasn't about to tell him her father would have a coronary. She *had* to show people, including her father, that she was capable of making her own decisions.

"Then what's the problem? I have plenty of space. I was going to suggest that you stay there anyway, until your ankle is healed. Lela, she's my house-keeper," he explained quickly, "will love having you." He flashed her another smile that made her stomach flutter. "Of course, she'll spoil you rotten." He saw she was struggling over the decision. It was obvious to him that she didn't like being in the position she was in. She was clearly the type who guarded her independence, perhaps as a result of being raised by an overprotective father. "Look, Roxie, it's my fault you have no money or transportation. I'd feel a hell of a lot better if you'd agree to stay at my place for a few days. If for no other reason than to assuage my guilt," he added.

Roxie pondered the offer. It made perfect sense. It was the only solution she could think of at the moment, and he *did* look as though he felt miserable about the whole thing. Not that he shouldn't feel guilty after having her car towed away in the first place, she decided. But how could she possibly sleep under the same roof with him, even for one night! Which was worse? she asked herself. Staying under the same roof with him, or becoming one of the wretched refuse of the streets? She lifted her chin a fraction. "Okay," she said in a voice that told him she wasn't too pleased. "I suppose I have no other choice."

He noticed the stubborn tilt of her chin and tried to suppress a smile. Spunky little thing, wasn't she? he thought. "Great," he said. "And in the meantime, I'll do everything possible to find your car." He turned toward a brass coatrack. "Mind if I change shirts before I drive you to my place?" When she merely shrugged, he reached for the hem of his T-shirt and pulled it over his head. Roxie found it impossible to look away. The muscles rippled in his arms as he casually stripped the stained garment from his body and hung it on the rack. His chest was wide, matted with black hair that grew sparse around his navel, which Roxie couldn't help but see because of his low-riding jeans. She felt her mouth go bone-dry. If this is what the man looked like from the waist up, she thought, she wouldn't *dare* imagine what he looked like from the waist down. She pried her gaze from his body and tried to fish her hairbrush from her purse with trembling hands to keep from gawking at him. She ran the brush through her hair quickly, then dropped it back into her purse.

"Ready?"

Roxie glanced up and found him completely dressed. Refusing to let him carry her again, she allowed him to put one of her arms around his shoulder so she could hobble along beside him. He curled his other arm around her waist to support her, then led her out and through the kitchen, where, thankfully, only a couple of employees were working. Roxie was glad they had the good manners to ignore her.

The sunlight blinded her for a moment when Tyler opened the back door, but she realized a car waited only a few feet away. Once they reached it, he let go of her long enough to unlock the door and open it. Gingerly he helped her in before closing the door. When he joined her in the front seat he noticed she was frowning. "Anything wrong?"

"Wouldn't you know it," she muttered. "You really *do* drive a Mercedes."

Three

It was more than half an hour later when Tyler pulled off the highway onto a private road. He and Roxie had conversed easily along the way, and she'd filled him in on all the gossip in Summerville. Although Tyler had severed all ties when he'd left twenty years before, he enjoyed listening as Roxie updated him on their hometown.

"How beautiful," Roxie said, once they'd gone a few miles down the road. Tall oaks lined the gravel drive they'd turned onto and in the distance she barely could make out a brick structure. When the trees finally opened into a clearing, a very large and imposing brick house stood before her. "This is where you live?" she asked in disbelief. He nodded as he parked in a circular drive that surrounded a garden which Roxie imagined had once been beautiful but had long since turned to weeds.

"I'm afraid it still needs a lot of work," he said, motioning toward the garden. "I've had a guy working on it since I bought it three years ago. He talks more than he works. He sort of reminds me of an older version of Mr. Haney on *Green Acres*."

Roxie laughed. "What's that?" she asked, when Tyler opened the door for her and helped her out. She pointed toward several crumbling brick buildings.

"Old slaves' quarters," he said, closing the door. "This used to be a pecan plantation. It's one of the few left in the South that still has the slaves' quarters standing. I'll show you around when your ankle heals." Tyler placed her arm around his shoulder and helped her toward the steps of the house. "Careful now," he said. "Take your time, we're not trying to win a race." Actually he liked being near her. Every once in a while he caught a whiff of her scent. He couldn't quite put a name to the fragrance, but he knew he would never tire of it.

Roxie took in the house with interest, despite being very much aware of the man beside her. "Do you still grow pecans?" she asked.

"Some. I use most of the land for grazing cattle, though. I supply my own beef for the restaurant."

"I'd love to have a look around sometime."

He gave her a patronizing smile. "Perhaps you'll have the chance, but for the next few days your behind will be planted in a chair." They had not quite made it to the front door before it was thrown open by a large, buxom woman wearing a white apron. Her hair was damp at the sides and pulled back in a knot at the nape of her neck, and her face was red and flushed as though she'd literally worked up a sweat.

"Oh, it's you," she said to Tyler, drying her hands on a dish towel. She tossed Roxie a questioning look.

"Lela, this is Miss Roxie Norris. She's going to be our house guest for a few days."

"What's wrong with her foot?" the woman asked, skipping the introductions.

Roxie gave her an apologetic look. "I'm afraid I sprained my ankle."

Lela stepped back and held the door for Tyler. "Well, don't just stand there like a bump on a log," she told him. "We need to get her off it right away." She assisted Tyler, and in a matter of seconds had Roxie sitting in a chair in a room they referred to as the den. It was large but cozy, the walls paneled in oak. A stone fireplace divided a wall filled with books. "Get that ottoman and prop her leg on it," Lela said to Tyler as she slipped a pillow behind Roxie's back. "How's that, honey? Are you comfortable?"

"Yes, thank you."

"Has a doctor looked at it?" Lela asked Tyler.

"Yes, Lela, I called one right away. He said Roxie would have to stay off her ankle for a couple of days."

"Did he X-ray it to make sure she had no broken bones?"

"No, I had him come directly to the restaurant."

"Then we have no way of knowing whether it's broken or not."

Roxie looked back and forth at the two as they argued. "It doesn't *feel* broken," she said.

"I'm sure the doctor would have insisted she go to the emergency room if he'd suspected a fracture," Tyler assured the older woman.

"Are you in pain?" Lela asked loudly, as though Roxie's sprained foot had somehow affected her hearing. But before she could answer, Tyler cut in.

"The doctor wrote out a prescription for a pain medication, but Roxie insisted she didn't need it."

"If you get to hurting, I'll give you something," Lela assured her. "You can buy it over the counter but it's good. Helps my arthritis." She looked at Tyler. "Why didn't you tell me you were bringing a guest home? I would have had the guest room all spiffy for her." When Tyler opened his mouth to answer, she cut him off. "And do you know you have to be back at the restaurant in less than one hour, and you haven't showered or eaten supper?"

"I can be late once in a while if I wish. I'm the boss, remember?" When she pursed her lips at him, he shrugged. "Okay, I'm going upstairs to shower right now." He headed toward the staircase, then paused and glanced at Roxie. "Just

make yourself at home. And if you need anything—"

"I'll take care of her if she needs anything," Lela
answered. As soon as Tyler had climbed the stairs,
Lela clucked her tongue sympathetically. "I'll bet
you're dying for a cool drink. Would you like a
glass of lemonade?"

"Yes, but I hate to put you to the trouble—"

"Don't you worry your pretty self about that,
now. As long as you're under this roof, you just
tell ol' Lela what you need, and it's as good as
done." Lela hurried away. Roxie leaned her head
back and closed her eyes. Somewhere in the house
she could hear water running and assumed Tyler
was taking his shower. Her overactive mind began conjuring up images of how he'd look—tall
and lean with water sluicing down his flat stomach. Her eyes flew open and she blushed in spite
of herself. Why couldn't she keep her mind off the
man's body, for heaven's sake? In fact, she realized, he'd been the perfect gentleman since he'd
learned who she was. He even had opened his
house to her.

"You look plum tuckered out," Lela said, coming into the room and breaking into Roxie's
thoughts. "I'm going upstairs right now to have a
look at the guest room. It shouldn't need more
than a little dusting. If Mr. Sheridan had called, it
would have been ready and waiting for you, but
you know how men are. They don't stop and think
about such things. That man wouldn't remember

to feed himself if I wasn't here to remind him. Know what I mean?" She didn't wait for Roxie to answer as she handed her a tall glass of lemonade. A second later, Roxie heard her climbing the stairs. She couldn't help the smile that twisted her lips, and for the first time in hours she completely forgot about her troubles.

Tyler came downstairs forty-five minutes later, freshly showered and dressed. Roxie did a double take. Gone were the tight jeans and grease-stained T-shirt he'd worn when they'd first met. Dressed in black slacks and a white dinner jacket, he looked as if he'd stepped straight out of *Casablanca*. Roxie realized her mouth was hanging open and she closed it.

"You look nice," she said. "More like you're going to a dinner party than to work, though."

Her compliment surprised him as much as it pleased him, and he hoped she wasn't merely being polite. During his shower, he had begun to wonder about her. Was there someone special in her life? Surely she wouldn't have been so eager to move to another city and leave a man behind. He was certain a woman with her looks would draw men like flies to a barbecue, but then there was her father to consider. In Summerville Reverend Norris was a monument to the people, serving as both dean and minister of one of the most prestigious Baptist colleges in the South. A suitor might feel intimidated by such a man, Tyler realized.

Roxie herself was an enigma. On the one hand

she appeared to be very prim and proper. On the other hand she could be a feisty little devil. But she'd had a temper even as a five-year-old, he remembered.

He thanked her for the compliment and helped her out of the chair. The tantalizing aroma of baked ham wafted through the house, but Roxie barely noticed—all she could smell was the sexy scent of Tyler's cologne. "I usually spend a couple of hours visiting with my regular customers," he said, explaining why he dressed as he did, "or welcoming newcomers. We usually have one or two VIPs present."

Roxie listened as he escorted her through an impressive dining room, where a chandelier hung over the table and was reflected in a wall-size mirror. She was thankful when Tyler pushed open a swinging door to the kitchen and she saw they were going to eat in a much smaller, more informal setting.

"I hope you don't mind eating in here," Tyler said. "I don't use the dining room unless I have a crowd coming."

"Actually I prefer this," Roxie said, hobbling beside him. She surveyed the old-fashioned kitchen. The white cabinets and light oak floors almost sparkled. Lela obviously took her job seriously. A fireplace dominated the wall beside the kitchen table, and she couldn't help but smile at the cozy picture it presented, so unlike how she'd visualized Tyler's home.

Lela glanced up from her place at the stove when they'd entered the room. "Miss Norris, you shouldn't be on that ankle. I was going to bring you a tray." She gave Tyler a look of reprimand. "You should have stopped her. I can't be everywhere at once." Tyler opened his mouth to speak, but Roxie beat him to it.

"It really doesn't hurt that much," Roxie said, "and I'd much prefer eating in here than in the den."

Lela's look softened. "If you're sure, honey. But I don't want you injuring yourself further. I hope you like baked ham. And I made potato salad and a nice gelatin dish that Mr. Sheridan especially likes. You know, it's so hot out, most folks don't have much of an appetite anyway." She talked nonstop as she served the food. Roxie glanced up and found Tyler smiling.

"She doesn't like you very much, does she?" Roxie whispered once Lela had served them and disappeared.

Tyler laughed. "That's just the way she is."

"You don't mind the way she lights into you now and then?"

"Actually I like it. Lela's been the closest thing to a mother I've ever had. Her own son died in Vietnam. Perhaps that's why we've grown so close over the past few years."

Roxie and Tyler finished the rest of their meal in comfortable silence. She couldn't help but wonder why a man like Tyler Sheridan didn't have a wife. He certainly had the looks and money to attract any woman he wanted—and that fact made her feel terribly uncomfortable. He was way out of her league. No doubt he dated sophisticated women. Women who were beautiful and witty and had all the qualities she lacked. She suddenly felt very self-conscious. He probably saw her as a first-rate hillbilly. Nevertheless, she couldn't control the flutter in her stomach or the way her pulse raced every time he gave her one of his knockout smiles. He probably did it on purpose just to take her unawares, she thought. And she'd be blind not to notice how his hair, wet from the shower, curled sensually at his forehead. His eyes could change in a flash from showing humor or concern to being downright sexy.

"I suppose you should telephone your father," Tyler suggested, tossing his napkin beside his plate once he'd finished eating. "Won't he worry if he doesn't hear from you?" He knew damn well her father would worry, but he couldn't tell her as much.

Roxie shrugged. "I'm sure he'll be okay." She didn't appreciate that Tyler presumed she had to check in with her father as though she were a child. And no matter how thoughtless her father would consider her if she didn't call, she decided she might as well set things straight from the beginning. She had moved away so he would recognize her independence, and that included not checking in with him on a daily basis.

Tyler was hesitant to say more. The last thing he wanted to do was arouse her suspicion. As it stood he could very well earn her trust and friendship and, maybe, as time went on, her confidence. He was going to have to proceed with caution. Although he'd already devised a few plans in the back of his mind, he wasn't about to move too quickly.

"Well, I'd better go," he said, wishing he didn't have to leave so soon. He wanted to stay and have a cup of coffee with Roxie on the porch and get to know her. He couldn't remember ever wanting to spend that kind of time with a woman before. Roxie didn't put on airs, and he liked that. She was simple and straightforward, and she looked as though she would welcome the company. No man in his right mind would turn down the chance to see dusk paint shadows on her face and to study her profile in the moonlight. Damn. He had to stop thinking of her romantically or he'd go crazy. "I'd better help you to your room first," he said a bit gruffly. "You look exhausted." When she opened her mouth to argue, he held up one hand. He was beginning to read her expressions, a thought he found endearing. "I'm not leaving until I help you to your room," he said. He stood and rounded the table, helping her to her feet. "Careful now," he said.

It took several minutes for them to make it through the house and up the stairs. They met Lela on the way. "Mr. Sheridan says you lost your luggage," she said, then glanced at Tyler. "I took the liberty of loaning Miss Norris a pair of your pajamas." She pursed her lips and gave Roxie a woman-to-woman look. "He don't wear them anyhow."

Roxie couldn't help but laugh at the woman's remark, and for a second, she thought she actually saw a slight blush on Tyler's face. Their gazes met and locked, and this time it was Roxie who blushed. Just thinking about Tyler Sheridan nude between the sheets sent her into a tizzy. Lord have mercy on her soul. Only a few hours with the man had reduced her to a sex maniac! All she could think about was his perfect face, wide chest, and those slim hips. "Thank you, Lela," Roxie said, trying to hide her discomfort. "And the name is Roxie, not Miss Norris."

Lela gave her a motherly smile and started down the stairs. "My bedroom is next to the kitchen," she said, "but I can hear everything that goes on in this house. You just give a holler, and I'll come running."

Roxie was very much aware of Tyler's broad hand at the small of her back as they climbed the stairs. "I hope you'll be comfortable in the guest room," he said, needing to break the silence between them. The act of leading her into the bedroom where she'd be sleeping made the moment intimate. His mind ran amok with the possibilities.

"I'm sure I will," she said, wishing he didn't have to rush off. They both seemed to feel awkward, Tyler because he didn't want to leave and Roxie because she didn't want him to. "May I pay you a compliment without sounding too personal?" she asked, a half smile playing on her lips.

He leaned against the doorjamb and grinned. "Lady, you can get as personal as you like."

She grinned back, but at the same time felt a warm blush on her cheeks. "I love your cologne," she said.

That brought a soft chuckle from him. "Good. I'm crazy about your perfume."

"And I really appreciate all you've done for me," she said. Balancing herself on her good foot, she stood on tiptoe and kissed him lightly on the cheek. Heaven help her, the man tasted as good as he looked!

She wasn't exactly sure who made the first move or how it happened, but the kiss, which had begun innocently enough, turned into something more. Tyler moved a fraction and their lips touched, briefly. Then suddenly his arms slipped around her waist and they were kissing—*really* kissing. His lips captured hers and sent her mind into a state of disarray. Roxie was lost and grasped the lapel of his jacket to keep from sinking to the floor. It was like riding a carnival's Tilt-a-whirl, she thought. Tyler broke the kiss and took a deep, shuddering breath. All they could do was stare at each other in amazement. What had obviously started out as a friendly kiss on her part had grown out of control. A raging forest fire, he thought, sensing she was as surprised as he by the intensity of it. It was as though her lips had been created specifically for his. The heavy pounding in his chest and the rush of desire in his loins frightened him.

"I have to go," he said, more to himself than to her. The last thing he wanted on his conscience was guilt over mauling his old friend's daughter inside his own house.

Roxie's thoughts were still scattered as a result of the kiss. "Good night, then," she finally said. She waited until he'd descended the stairs and let himself out the front door before she budged.

Roxie opened the bedroom door to find a lovely four-poster bed topped with a blue and white comforter that matched the curtains billowing out from the window with the breeze. A ceiling fan whirled over her bed, making the room comfortably cool. A small portable television sat in one corner of the room, and a bookshelf loaded with paperbacks in the other. She opened a door that led to a bathroom and decided to take a long bath, then curl up in bed with a book until she got sleepy. It was still early, she realized, but she was tired after the day's mishaps.

She smiled at the window seat and settled herself in it to gaze out at the rolling, lush, green countryside. Roxie pressed her cheek against the screen and caught the faint scent of honeysuckle. A light breeze rustled through a live oak near her window.

But Roxie's thoughts were not entirely captured by the lovely surroundings. Tyler Sheridan had kissed her. True, she had kissed him first, but she never had expected him to respond with such fervor. And she never had expected her own body to go ignite as a result. She touched one finger to her lips and wondered if she would ever be the same again.

"She's fine, really" Tyler tried to assure the man on the other end of the line. Roxie's father had called earlier and left a message for Tyler to return the call as soon as possible. "She just sprained her ankle, that's all. The doctor bandaged it and told her to stay off it for a few days." Tyler wasn't about to tell the man about the robbery or Roxie's car. Her father probably would get into his own car that very night and drive to Charleston. "Where is she staying?" Tyler said, repeating the question the minister had asked. He hesitated. "I insisted she stay at my place where my housekeeper can look after her. At least until she can get around," he added, feeling guilty as hell for having kissed her so passionately. He didn't know what had possessed him to do such a thing. "Oh, it's no trouble," he insisted when the man on the other end apologized for the imposition. "My housekeeper will pamper her as if she were a new kitten."

Tyler was thankful when he hung up a few minutes later. He sat at his desk for several minutes thinking about the conversation that had taken place. He was the middleman in a situation he didn't like one bit. On one hand, he could understand a father's concern for his daughter. On the other hand, he certainly could understand Roxie's desire to be on her own. After all, she was a grown woman. If he had doubted it before, she had proved him wrong in his arms.

But he owed the man, dammit! If it hadn't been for Roxie's father, he'd probably be in prison. Roxie's father had helped him find a new life, a very successful life. He had no choice but to repay the favor. It was the right choice, he decided. It was the *only* choice.

So why was he feeling like such a snitch?

The following morning Roxie found her luggage at the foot of the stairs. She smiled shyly as she limped into the kitchen, where the aroma of fresh coffee and eggs and bacon enticed her. Lela was at the stove, and Tyler was sipping coffee as he scribbled something on a slip of paper.

"Good morning," she said, feeling self-conscious in Tyler's oversize pajamas, which she had rolled up at the arms and legs. She found it difficult to make eye contact with him after what had happened between them the night before. She had lain awake long afterward wondering about the kiss. She had finally convinced herself that while the earth may have moved for her, it was probably no big deal for Tyler Sheridan. She had decided to pretend it never happened. It wouldn't be easy, of course. Every time she looked into those gorgeous brown eyes she would remember the kiss. But she could act as cool as the next person if she had to.

"Mornin'," Tyler said, looking up. He grinned at the sight of her in his pajamas.

"How did you get down those stairs by yourself?" Lela said. "You should have called someone to help you."

"Actually my ankle feels much better this morning," Roxie told her, thankful the woman was present and she and Tyler weren't alone. "In fact, I don't see why I should even bother with this bandage." She took a seat next to Tyler, and Lela hurried over with a cup of coffee.

"Don't be in such a hurry to get rid of that bandage," Lela said. "You could end up hurting yourself worse. Why, I once had this cousin . . ." Lela began a lengthy story about a man who'd started off with a simple sprained ankle, only to have his foot amputated in the end.

Roxie sipped her coffee as she listened wide-eyed to Lela. She glanced at Tyler, who merely shook his head and rolled his eyes as though warning Roxie not to believe everything Lela told her. "Why, that's just awful," Roxie said, once Lela had finished her story. "What happened to him after that?"

"Oh, he's dead now," Lela said. "He got kicked in the head by a mule a couple of years later." Lela set a plate heaped with eggs and grits and bacon before her.

"Lela, I can't possibly eat all this," Roxie said. "Anyway, I usually don't eat breakfast."

"You do now," the large woman told her. "You're as skinny as a bean pole. I told Mr. Sheridan that's why you hadn't found yourself a husband, 'cause you was just too blasted bony." Tyler laughed out loud at the comment, and Roxie shot him an indignant look.

"It just so happens I've had one or two marriage proposals over the years," she told him coolly.

"Then how come you haven't taken someone up on it?" he asked.

"Because I don't want to live under the thumb of some man, that's why. I enjoy my freedom. I like to come and go as I please." He shrugged and went back to his writing. Lela muttered something about having to put in a load of laundry and left the room. Roxie buttered a slice of toast and glanced at Tyler. "What are you writing?"

"I'm going to advertise in the newspaper for a waitress. I'm rather shorthanded right now."

"Oh?" Roxie continued eating in silence. "Does the job pay well?" she asked after a moment.

"Waitresses make pretty good tips. Some make as much as a hundred bucks a night—more on weekends," he added.

"Really? Do you need experience?"

"Oh, yeah," he said, nodding his head. "Unless, of course, I knew someone could do the job. Then I'd have one of my best waitresses train her."

Roxie was thoughtful for a moment. "How about

me?" she asked. When Tyler gave her a blank look, she continued. "I mean, do you think I could do the work?"

He chuckled. "I doubt it, Red. The work is pretty hard. The girls clock in at five-thirty in the afternoon and don't get out until after one o'clock in the morning."

"Yes, but they make good money, right?" She paused. "I'm not afraid of hard work, Tyler. And I learn fast."

"I don't know," he said, shaking his head doubtfully.

She was growing impatient. "Look, we're both in a bind, right? I need money fast and you need a waitress. In a few days, I'd have enough money to rent an apartment. Nothing fancy, mind you, but at least I'd be on my own. What do you say?"

"How do you plan to get to work? This house isn't on the bus line, you know. Which reminds me. Once the police located your car, I had my mechanic go over it. He should be able to tell you what's wrong."

"Oh." Her heart sank. There was no telling what was wrong with her car, what it would cost to repair, or how long it would take to save the money. "I could ride with you," she said hopefully. "Of course, I'd pay for half the gas."

"You wouldn't have to pay for gas," he said. "I have to drive back and forth anyway."

"I insist. I won't take no for an answer."

He sighed. "Okay, Red. Whatever you say. You can start next Monday. That'll give you today, tomorrow, and the weekend to stay off your ankle. I'll take you in early on Monday to be fitted for a uniform."

She smiled. "You won't regret this, Tyler. I promise to do my best." She toasted him with her coffee cup.

Tyler wadded up the piece of paper he'd been scribbling on, stood, and carried it over to the trash can. He tossed it in, feeling proud of himself. His plan had worked, and it had been easier than he'd thought.

He felt guilty as hell.

Four

The following morning Roxie decided to do some exploring even though Lela used every excuse known to man to keep her off her ankle. But after spending the previous day cooped up inside the house listening to Clem, the carpenter, either drilling or hammering, Roxie was determined to get out. As she slipped out the back door, she ran into Tyler, who was coming from the direction of the barn.

"Where do you think you're going?" he asked, frowning as Lela had only moments before.

"I need fresh air," Roxie told him matter-of-factly. She saw him glance at her bare legs and felt uncomfortable in her shorts, but it was impossible to get a pair of jeans over her Ace bandage. The way he looked at her made her think of the kiss again, and her stomach fluttered as it always did when her thoughts traveled in that direction.

"I thought we agreed you would stay off your ankle so it would heal by the time you started work on Monday." He pried his gaze from her legs and forced himself to look stern.

"I never agreed to such a thing," she said. "All I agreed to do was wear the bandage until Monday. Besides, it's only a minor sprain." Darn it, why was she trying to defend herself to the man? And why did he seem to have such an uncanny knack of making her feel like a child? It infuriated her. She may owe him her gratitude for his help, but she certainly didn't owe him an explanation for everything she did.

"Suit yourself," he said, muttering a curse under his breath. He jerked the back door open and let the screen slam behind him. Lela shot him a questioning look.

"What has you so riled up this morning?" she asked, wiping her hands on her apron and going to the refrigerator. She reached inside for a pitcher of lemonade and poured him a tall glass.

He grunted in response and thanked her when she handed him the glass. He was acting like an idiot, he told himself. But then, why did Roxie have to go prancing around half dressed, for pete's sake? The hammering upstairs set him on edge. He glared at Lela. "When in the hell is that man going to be finished working on this house?"

Lela shrugged. "How should I know, he doesn't work for me. I told you when you hired him he belonged in a nursing home. He's too old to be doing that kind of work."

"Well, this place could have been finished long ago if the man were competent."

"Then how come you don't fire him and stop chewing *my* head off?"

Tyler raked his fingers through his hair when he realized they were shouting at each other. "I'm sorry," he said, feeling as edgy as a treed coon. "I hired him because he needed the job." He took a sip of the cold drink. "Aw, hell, I can't stand the noise any longer." He set the glass down with a loud thump and stalked toward the back door.

"You could always take a cold shower," Lela said, giving him a knowing look.

Tyler came to an abrupt halt at the back door. "What?"

"I've seen the way you look at her. A soul would be blind not to notice."

Tyler gaped at the woman. "You don't know what you're talking about." He slammed out the door as Lela stood chuckling at the sink.

Tyler found Roxie talking to his hired hand, Rusty Sparks, who obviously had just saddled one of the horses. He appeared to be answering questions about the animal. Roxie rubbed the mare above her nose and stroked her sleek neck affectionately. Watching her run her graceful hands over the animal's shiny coat made Tyler's own flesh itch. He gritted his teeth when he saw the appreciative glances Rusty gave her.

"I thought you were going out to look for that

new calf," Tyler said, walking toward the two of them, his forehead creased in a frown. If Roxie wanted to strut her stuff, she could do it inside and stay away from his men, he decided. Not that Rusty could be labeled a man; he still had a year to go in high school.

"I was just going," Rusty said. He swung himself into the saddle and touched the brim of his old baseball cap. "Nice meetin' you, Miss Norris. I hope you enjoy your stay."

"Thanks, Rusty. And please call me Roxie."

Tyler pressed his lips together with growing irritation. The boy couldn't keep his eyes off her. He nodded once more at Roxie and prodded the mare forward. Roxie turned to Tyler with a bright smile.

"That's a beautiful animal. Do you own many horses?"

"I own enough," he said bluntly. "Next time you want to have a look at my livestock, I would appreciate your coming to me. I'm not paying my men to stand around and ogle you."

Her mouth fell open in surprise. "Ogle me?"

"And don't pretend you don't know what I'm talking about. You know perfectly well what you're doing; otherwise you wouldn't be dressed that way." His gaze took in the tank top she was wearing. Her breasts were full and round, her nipples tiny little nodes that strained against the fabric. She wasn't wearing a bra, he noted. *She wasn't wearing a bra!*

Roxie felt her temper rise. "Forgive me. I had no

idea your men were so lustful. And I thought since the weather was so warm, I wouldn't wear my sackcloth and ashes today." She turned on her heels and her ponytail almost slapped him in the face.

Tyler suddenly realized how ridiculous he was being, but, dammit, he thought, he didn't enjoy seeing men leer at her. And that was twice as ridiculous, because he had no claim on her. "Roxie, wait—" Tyler grabbed her wrist. She jerked free. "Look, I'm sorry, okay?" She walked toward the house, her head held high, her chin thrust forward impudently. He sighed inwardly, watching her. The shorts molded perfectly against her swaying hips, making his gut wrench with desire. She threw open the screen door with a vengeance. He was half afraid she was going to rip it off the hinges. Damn, she had a temper! He watched the door slam behind her, and he stalked off with his fists clenched by his sides.

Lela was standing at the kitchen sink when Roxie entered the room in a huff. "I see you met Rusty," Lela said, glancing out the window in front of her. "He's such a nice boy. I've known that young'un since he was in diapers. Me and his mama have been friends for years. 'Course, his daddy wasn't worth ten cents, if you ask me. Sorriest man I ever laid eyes on. He's dead now, Lord rest his unworthy soul."

Roxie blinked, knowing she was in for a long story.

"Pardon me, Lela," Roxie said as politely as she

could, "but do you happen to have an old dress I could borrow?"

Lela glanced at her in surprise. "Honey, all I got is old dresses. Why?"

"I'd like to borrow one, if I may."

"What are you planning to do with it?"

"Wear it."

Lela frowned. "Wear it? But you'd get lost in one of my dresses."

Roxie crossed her arms over her breasts. "Precisely."

Twenty minutes later, Roxie made her way outside wearing one of Lela's oldest dresses, a navy blue paisley print. The shoulders were twice the width of her own, and the only thing holding the garment on her body was the belt she'd put around her waist. The dress hung to her ankles, revealing very little of the bandage she wore, or her socks and sneakers. Surely she wouldn't tempt a man now, she told herself.

She strode briskly and purposefully toward the barn, and from the corner of her eye, saw Tyler standing beside the barbed-wire fence talking to another hired hand. She smiled with satisfaction, realizing the picture she must present.

The barn was dark and cool and smelled of fresh hay. Roxie passed through it, glancing curiously into the stalls at the horses. She paused and reached out to stroke a spotted one near the end of the barn and smiled when the horse snorted and backed away. "Easy now," she whispered. "I won't hurt you. If you're nice, perhaps I'll bring a sugar cube next time." The horse stared at her doubtfully.

"Just what the hell do you think you're doing?"

Roxie feigned a look of surprise. "I'm trying to pet one of your horses. Should I have asked first?" It was difficult to maintain her composure. Standing at the barn door silhouetted by the afternoon sun, Tyler made a striking figure of a man. Roxie found it impossible to keep her gaze off him as he closed the distance between them in his long-legged stride. He looked as powerful as the animals she had been admiring.

Tyler walked toward her. She was deliberately goading him, but he would never have guessed as much by the innocent look on her face. Her ponytail, which he thought endearing, if not downright cute, was now twisted into a severe knot at the back of her neck. Her legs and derriere, which had teased him almost into a state of arousal only moments before, were now buried under yards of material. Instead of bursting into laughter as he was tempted to do, he tried to appear serious. "Now that's more like it," he said, nodding his head in approval at her attire as he came to a stop in front of her. He saw a look of disbelief cross her face. "You look the perfect lady, if you don't mind my saying so." Actually, she looked beguiling as hell, he thought. The dress had slipped off one shoulder, exposing her silky smooth skin. He couldn't help but wonder how her skin would feel and taste beneath a man's lips—*his* lips. Even though her face radiated sweetness and innocence, it was the face of a mature woman. Her lips were full and sensual, her jaw delicate. He longed to trace the lines of her face with his tongue. Her eyes, even in anger, were mystical and made him want to gaze deeper into them. Who was Roxie Norris? he wondered. And when had nature decided to do away with the tangled hair and skinned knees, and paint such a tempting picture?

Roxie knew he was making fun of her. Her plan had failed miserably. She had hoped to make him see how ridiculous he had been; instead, he was complimenting her. "I'm glad you approve," she said coolly. "I certainly don't want your men to think your house guest is a floozy." She felt like a fool but realized she probably looked one as well. All she wanted to do was go to her room and lock the door behind her. But she'd be darned if she'd let Tyler see her plan had backfired. "Now, if you'll excuse me—" She started to walk away, but Tyler's arm shot out and stopped her.

"There's only one problem with the dress," Tyler said. "The shoulders are much too wide." As if to prove his point, he reached out and pulled the material back in place. His knuckles skidded across her warm skin, and his insides seemed to turn over. How was a man supposed to ignore the fact that she was beautiful and tempting? And what man in his right mind could overlook a face such as hers and remain loyal to an old friend? At that moment he almost despised the good reverend for sending his daughter to him.

As if acting out a dream, Tyler let one callused hand glide across her shoulder and up the side of her neck. He was so lost in his own thoughts, he didn't see the astonishment in her eyes.

Roxie felt as though her heart were about to leap from her chest. She was certain he could hear it beating as he traced the delicate line of her collarbone with his thumb. His sooty eyelids were heavy, his eyes glazed as though he were entranced. He surprised her further when he leaned forward and pressed his lips into the hollow of her shoulder, sending chills dancing along her spine. Roxie heard a sigh of pleasure leave her. He nibbled his way up her neck and found her earlobe and nipped it gently, while one finger idly traced the sensitive skin along her inner arm. Roxie shivered at the prickling sensations that followed.

His lips moved from the shell of her ear to the base of her throat, then inched up her neck. He hesitated only a second before capturing her mouth in a heated kiss. Roxie felt her knees buckle beneath her. She clutched the front of his cotton shirt frantically and heard him moan in response.

Tyler knew he was losing control, felt it in the bulge that pressed against the zipper of his jeans. He could easily pull her down in an empty stall and make love to her. He wouldn't have to undress her, he told himself. He merely would push the dress up her thighs and . . . He froze suddenly at his own thoughts. He raised his lips from hers and stared at her in disbelief. Suddenly he went cold all over, realizing what he'd been thinking. Her lips were swollen and damp from his kisses, and he wanted to go on kissing her.

Tyler released her with a force that would have sent her sprawling had she not fallen against the stall. He raked his hands through his hair, trying to come up with a feasible explanation for what he'd done. "I apologize for what just happened," he said gruffly. "I don't know what came over me." It was a lame excuse, but the only one he had.

"Neither do I," she said, gazing up at him, half dazed. Frankly she felt wonderful being in his arms. "But I thought it was nice."

Nice, hell, he thought. Holding her was sheer heaven. He could imagine what it would be like to have her naked in his bed with her red hair fanned across his pillow. He could lose himself in her eyes and that hair and the taste of her mouth. Damn, why was he allowing himself even to think along those lines?

"Roxie, I owe you an apology," he said, realizing how unreal his voice sounded to his own ears. She opened her mouth to speak, and he pressed one finger against her lips. "Listen to me," he insisted. "I'm not right for you. You need a man who can love you and give himself to you for the rest of your life. Someone who can give you children and a normal life. I'm not that man, Roxie." Besides, he only was fulfilling an obligation, he reminded himself. Once her new job began, he wouldn't have to worry about her anymore. He almost hated himself for agreeing to look after her in the first place.

Roxie crossed her arms and glared at him. "Who do you think you are, Tyler Sheridan, telling me what I need and don't need? I'm capable of making my own decisions, thank you." She didn't give him a chance to answer. "You're the one who doesn't know your own mind. One minute you're kissing me as though you can't get enough, the next thing I know you're backing off as though I've got the plague. Why don't you make up your mind, for heaven's sake?" Without another word, she whirled around, her skirt flying, and hurried out of the barn.

Tyler stood there a long time afterward, trying to get his emotions, not to mention his physical state, under control. Beads of perspiration popped out on his forehead and upper lip. He kicked the stall with his boot and sent the horse on the other side skittering. He cursed his own behavior, then spent the next fifteen minutes calming the animal.

Tyler did not appear at breakfast the following morning, and when Roxie questioned Lela, she learned he had not come home all night. Roxie's heart sank with the news. She'd spent much of the night thinking about what had happened in the barn the day before and had purposely dressed to please Tyler. Her knee-length khaki shorts looked conservative with a crisp, white short-sleeve blouse.

"Friday and Saturday nights are his busiest," Lela said. "He sometimes sleeps at the restaurant."

Roxie nodded as though it made good sense, but couldn't stop wondering whether he had spent the night alone. They had both done their best to avoid each other once they'd left the barn. Roxie had returned Lela's dress and had helped the woman around the house.

She and Lela had become friends right away, and Roxie was thankful since she didn't know anyone in Charleston. Still, she thought, the house seemed empty without Tyler. The weekend promised to be very dull.

Roxie rinsed her dishes and placed them in the dishwasher. She refused to let Lela wait on her. She propped her elbows on the sink and stared out the window at nothing in particular. It was going to be another hot day. She had spotted Rusty on horseback earlier, and thought he probably was checking to see that all was well with the cattle. "Lela, what's that building over the garage?" Roxie asked in a bored tone.

Lela, who was busy mixing ingredients for a cake, looked up. "Right now it's used for storage," the woman said. "Before that it was the servants' quarters. That was long before Mr. Sheridan bought the place."

"Really? Think I could have a look?"

"Why? Do you feel a sudden need to get filthy?" the woman asked. "That place ain't nothing but a dust bowl. But suit yourself. The keys are over by the back door."

Roxie hurried over and found several sets of keys hanging from a wooden key rack. A small strip of masking tape identified each, and she reached for the one she needed. "I'll be back in a minute," she told Lela. The woman nodded and smiled. It was obvious she had given up trying to make Roxie stay off her ankle.

Roxie climbed the stairs next to the garage. Once she'd unlocked the door, she pushed it open and stepped inside.

Sunlight streamed through the open door, as dust motes scattered in a hundred different directions. Roxie blinked several times before her eyes adjusted to the dim room. Furniture covered with white sheets filled the room to capacity. Several metal filing cabinets stood off to one side, as well as boxes of every shape and size.

Roxie weaved her way through the clutter and found a small old-fashioned kitchen. Although it was in dire need of a coat of paint, the cabinets, countertops, and linoleum floor were in good shape. She made her way through the rest of the apartment. The bathroom, complete with a claw-foot bathtub and pedestal sink, looked as though it hadn't been cleaned in a coon's age. The linoleum was worn and curled at the edges, and Roxie was certain she had never seen uglier wallpaper.

She continued her tour, opening doors to two large bedrooms. When she returned to the living room, she glanced beneath the sheets at the furniture and saw several couches, tables, mismatched chairs, and dressers. Although unattractive, the furniture seemed serviceable. Roxie sank into an overstuffed chair and began to plan.

When Tyler returned home shortly before lunch, Roxie was waiting for him. He hadn't slept well on the couch in his office, but it had been safer than sleeping under the same roof with her. After what happened between them the day before, he was determined to keep his distance.

"Tyler, I've come up with a wonderful idea," she said as Lela served them sandwiches and iced tea. She forced herself to maintain eye contact, despite the fact every time she looked at him she thought of the scene they'd made in the barn. Both Tyler and Lela shot her a questioning look. "I'd like to move into the servants' quarters," she said matter-of-factly.

Lela was the first to object. "Honey, you can't do that. That place is a mess."

"I know, but I can spend the weekend fixing it up," she replied. "All it really needs is a good scrubbing, some paint, and wallpaper. Have you seen how much paint Clem ordered to finish the rooms in this house? There will be plenty to do both the house *and* the apartment."

"And just what do you plan to do with the furniture and other items being stored in there?" Tyler asked.

"Simple. Since I'll only need one bedroom, everything else can be stored in the spare bedroom.

Rusty even agreed to help me move the furniture this afternoon."

"Oh, that was grand of him," Tyler muttered, then took a bite of his sandwich. When he'd finished swallowing, he went on. "And who's going to help Rusty move all that furniture?"

Roxie didn't hesitate. "I am. I offered Rusty five dollars an hour to help me." When Tyler didn't answer right away, she became insistent. "Well, what do you think?" He remained silent. "Look, if you're worried about the money, I'll pay rent just as soon as I start waitressing at the restaurant."

"You think I'd actually charge you to live in that place?" he asked in disbelief.

"Of course," she said, equally surprised. "Why not?"

"Because it's a dump, that's why."

"Not for long," she said brightly, noticing that Lela was frowning at the idea. She sobered instantly. "Listen, Tyler, I really can make it livable. I know I can. I can sew. Once I make new curtains and paint the place, you won't recognize it. My only other alternative is to move to the YWCA."

"What's so bad about staying here?" he said, glancing around the kitchen.

"I can't live here. I need my own place. Besides, I'll only need the apartment temporarily. Once my new job starts, I'll have to move closer to the university. If I fix the place up, you'll be able to rent the apartment to someone else after I'm gone."

Tyler shook his head. The lady was truly an enigma. "Okay, do what you want," he said. "But

I don't expect you to pay rent. At least not while you're remodeling the place," he added, knowing she'd argue the point till he was gray. "And I'll cover the expenses. If you can't find decent furniture there or in the attic here, I'll buy what you need."

"The furniture won't be a problem, but I'll need cleaning supplies and paint." She would worry about material for curtains later.

"Lela, will you see that Roxie has all she needs?" Tyler asked.

Lela nodded but still looked doubtful. "I should have enough cleaning supplies."

Tyler finished his sandwich. "What time is Rusty planning to help you move the furniture?" he asked Roxie, who appeared to be very pleased at the moment.

"Right after lunch. He said he only works half days on Saturday."

"Okay, tell him I'll be out shortly. You already have a sprained ankle, I certainly don't want to deal with a broken back." When she started to argue, he cut her off. "Either we do it my way or not at all."

Roxie closed her mouth, thankful for her one small victory. She felt Tyler's gaze on her as she carried her plate to the sink, rinsed it, and loaded it into the dishwasher before going out the back door.

Tyler wanted to smile but realized Lela was watching. He had suspected Roxie wouldn't hang around, no matter how broke she was. And he knew without asking that she'd never take a dime from him. He had wondered all along where Roxie was going to choose to live and how he would be able to keep an eye on her. He knew he couldn't live too close to her and still keep his sanity.

Roxie had settled the problem on her own, and now he questioned why he hadn't thought of it himself.

Five

It took Tyler and Rusty three hours to move the furniture and other items into the extra bedroom. Roxie spent the time scrubbing away years of dirt and grime from the kitchen and bathroom. She had chosen the furniture she would need, and although some of the pieces weren't bad, the upholstery was worn and faded. Tyler offered to have the furniture redone, but she refused.

"They'll do," she said, waving the matter aside. The important thing was that she wouldn't be living under the same room with Tyler Sheridan.

Once the men had finished, Roxie pulled out her wallet and held out fifteen dollars to Rusty. He blushed profusely. "I didn't do it for the money, Miss Norris." He backed toward the door as she followed him, insisting he take the money. The more she argued, the more embarrassed Rusty became.

"He doesn't want the money, Roxie," Tyler finally said in exasperation. "Now would you please put it away and let the poor boy go."

Roxie thanked Rusty and stood at the door until he cleared the steps. When she came back inside, she was thoughtful. "I know what I'll do. I'll buy him some cologne."

Tyler frowned. She certainly didn't seem concerned about all the work *he'd* done. "I'm going to finish setting up that iron bedstead," he muttered, stalking toward the bedroom. But the whole time he worked, he kept thinking how Roxie would look curled up on the bed.

Roxie was trying to decide what to do with the wood floors when Lela knocked on the door, carrying an armload of sheets and towels. She even had a couple of pillows. "It's old stuff," she explained, "but they will serve their purpose. I also found some old dishes and pots and pans in the attic. I'll ask Mr. Sheridan to carry them over for you." She set the things down and ventured into the kitchen. "Looks like somebody's been working," she said. She took a quick tour of the rest of the apartment and grinned at Roxie as they watched Tyler trying to put the old iron bed together, muttering obscenities as he worked.

"Guess what else I found in the attic?" Lela said, once they'd left Tyler alone with his work. "A sewing machine. You could use it to make your curtains."

"Who's going to carry it down from the attic and up these stairs?" Roxie asked. Both women glanced in the direction of the bedroom, where Tyler continued to mutter under his breath. "Maybe we shouldn't rush into it," Roxie said.

Lela nodded. "We'll give it a few days."

Tyler made his way down the hall, wiping sweat from his brow. His clothes were a mess. "I wouldn't open the door to that spare bedroom if I were you," he told Roxie. "We had to stack furniture on top of other furniture to make it all fit. If you open that door, you might start an avalanche." When Roxie nodded, he glanced around the room. It wasn't the Ritz but it would do, he supposed. "Is there anything else you need before I take my shower?" Roxie was about to say no when Lela interrupted.

"Mr. Sheridan, there *is* one itty-bitty thing you can do," she said hurriedly. "I found a couple of boxes of old dishes and pots and pans in the attic. I think Roxie can use them." She glanced at Roxie. " 'Course, none of them match, but I don't reckon you'll be having the President and his wife over for dinner any time soon. There's some silverware in one of the boxes as well," she added.

Tyler made his way out the door, mumbling under his breath again. "I wish you hadn't asked him to do that," Roxie said. "I could have done it myself."

"Oh, he doesn't mind," Lela assured her. "He may look miserable, but believe me, he wouldn't have set foot in here unless he wanted to help.

Well, I'd best get back to the house and check on supper. Are you planning to eat at the house?"

Roxie shook her head. "No, I'm going to keep working. I only have tonight and tomorrow to get this place livable before I start my new job."

"Well, I'll bring over a plate later," Lela said, letting herself out the door. "You're going to have to keep up your strength if you plan to get this place in order." She rolled her eyes as Roxie laughed.

Tyler made three trips from the attic to Roxie's new apartment, hauling all the items Lela had pointed out. Sweat seeped from every pore of his body. Why in heaven's name he was doing all this work was beyond him. He could have *hired* somebody to do it. But just seeing the smile on Roxie's face each time he dropped off another box raised his spirits enormously. It was as though he delivered treasure—not mismatched, chipped dishes.

He was huffing and puffing by the time he carried in the last box. Roxie already had run a sinkful of hot soapy water and loaded most of the dishes into it. "That's the last of it," he said, leaning against the door frame in the kitchen. She was up to her elbows in suds. A dark smudge on the tip of her nose suddenly captivated him, and he was tempted to brush it away. For a moment all he could do was watch her. "Are you sure you want to sleep here tonight?" he asked, glancing around the place, trying to keep his eyes off her. Her shorts, although they were a respectable length, emphasized her slender waist and pert derrière. He kept his gaze trained on his surroundings. She had made monumental improvements in the apartment in just a few short hours, but it would take weeks to do all the work and painting needed. "There's a lot left to do," he said, voicing the thought aloud. "You could always come back in the morning."

For a moment he regretted letting her have the apartment. At the time it had been the answer to his problems. He wouldn't have to lie awake at night and think about her sleeping in the room down the hall. He wouldn't be haunted by her perfume or the sound of her voice as she talked with Lela, or Clem. But now he was beginning to think he'd made a mistake. His house would seem empty without her. In a couple of days, she had turned it into a home, with her smiles and laughter. He envied her zest for life. Somewhere along the way he had gotten into a rut. His world had revolved around the Southern Belle for so long, little time remained for anything else.

Roxie pondered his suggestion. Although she was tired and knew there was a lot to do before she could climb into bed, she felt it best to stay put. "Thanks for the offer, Tyler, but I think I'll go ahead and sleep here tonight." She smiled to break the sudden tension in the air. His face was creased with dust and sweat, and he had never looked more handsome to her.

"I really appreciate all you've done for me, though." The last time she'd said those words, she had stood on tiptoe to kiss him, and he had taken her in his arms and kissed her soundly.

"Well . . ." He paused, not wanting to leave yet, but knowing he had to shave and shower and get to the restaurant. Damn, he thought. He'd let some woman, his friend's daughter, step in and turn his world upside down. But he couldn't resist reaching over finally and wiping the smudge from her upturned nose. She laughed.

"I'm going to have to soak in a hot tub for an hour to get the grime off me."

Tyler almost groaned at the thought of her sitting nude in the antique bathtub filled with water. Her skin would be a rosy pink in the steaming water, and her thighs . . . Dammit to hell! He was doing it again. "I have to go now," he said abruptly. "Otherwise I'll be late." He swiveled and headed for the door without another word.

Roxie arched her brows as she reached for a dish towel and dried her hands quickly, trying to catch up with him. "Tell you what," she said brightly. "Once I get settled, I'm going to invite you to dinner." He pushed the door open, and she had to jump to catch it before it slammed in her face. "I'm not a bad cook. Not as good as Lela, but—" She paused and frowned. "Tyler?"

He stopped halfway down the stairs and turned around. "What?" He growled the word.

"What's wrong?"

He laughed out loud at the question, but it wasn't a happy sound. Was the woman blind, for pete's sake? "What's wrong?" he asked in disbelief. Didn't she realize how she tempted him, even in his dreams? he wondered. His eyes flashed irritation, but what irked him most was the fact that he couldn't seem to pry his gaze from the top button on her blouse. A wisp of lace peered out from her collar, just enough to tantalize him and make him want to see more. Beneath that willful and spunky facade was a very feminine woman, whose body was designed for a man's hands. He ached to feel the weight of her breasts in each of his palms and to flick the dusky nipples with his tongue until they quivered. His imagination ran wild with the possibilities, until he literally was trembling with need and frustration. She was the forbidden fruit, and like Adam in the Garden of Eden, he found the temptation too great.

"You want to know what's wrong?" He retraced his steps, pulled her inside the apartment, and took her in his arms. Roxie stiffened in surprise, but as his mouth captured hers and his tongue foraged its way inside, she felt her resistance slip away, and she became warm and pliant in his arms. In a matter of seconds she was responding eagerly. Her body had taken control.

Tyler kissed her deeply, urgently, whispering her name as they both gasped for air. "This is what's wrong, Red," he confessed. He gazed down at her, awed by the picture she presented. His emotions surfaced and blocked out common sense. Once again his mouth came down on hers, hard and eager. There would be time for guilt and retribution later, but for now all he could think of was holding her, tasting her, and inhaling her sweetness. He whispered her name as his lips drifted from her mouth to her neck. In a daze, he realized she was whispering his name as well. He reached around and cupped her hips in his hands and pulled her up against him, cradling her against his hardness and swaying gently to the rhythm of their heartbeats.

Roxie looked up at him with passion-glazed eyes. She wasn't thinking, she was reacting. He ground his hardness against her until she gasped and clung to him tightly, wanting to experience all he had to offer. It was frightening and wonderful at the same time. While one part of her was eager to know him fully, another part shied away. What power did this man wield that she could suddenly turn away from all that was ingrained in her? Why did she feel a wild reckless heat in her veins every time he touched her? No man ever had aroused such feelings in her before. Surely there was more to it than mere lust.

Suddenly Roxie's ardor matched his own. She pulled his head down and kissed him, her tongue seeking his once again. Their breathing was raspy and hot. Tyler took her bottom lip between his teeth and nipped it, all the while moving sensually against her. Roxie could feel the warmth spread from her lower belly to her thighs. There had to be an end to this sweet misery, and she knew it rested with him.

"Have you ever wanted somebody so bad it hurt?" he asked her, his words barely audible against her lips. "I wanted to make love to you the first time I saw you," he said.

"I want you to make love to me too, Tyler," she said truthfully, her body sensitized to his every touch. "But I'm not . . . prepared."

Tyler continued to kiss her, his mouth so hungry for the taste of her flesh, he couldn't think straight. When he raised his gaze to hers, he appeared confused. "What do you mean you're not prepared?"

She glanced away, feeling totally inadequate. She was a woman of the eighties, she should have been prepared. "I don't have any means of birth control," she confessed, feeling like an idiot. For the first time in her life, she wanted to give herself to a man—this man. She wanted to yield to him completely, mate with him, and feel his powerful arms and thighs around her. And yet she was not prepared, had never been prepared for such a moment. She wanted to die.

Tyler could almost hear the iron bars slam down between them. He gazed at her. "You're a virgin." It wasn't a question, it was a statement, and something in her eyes told him he spoke the truth. He suddenly felt very foolish, pressed against her intimately. He pulled himself free and staggered backward. "Roxie, I'm sorry. I should have known. I mean, hell, I should have suspected as much, but the way you responded to me . . ." He saw tears glistening in her eyes and his heart turned over in his chest. "Oh, Lord, Red." He pulled her into his arms and held her. It took every ounce of will-power he had to hold back his desire.

How long they stood there, Tyler wasn't sure. Their breathing had returned to normal, but he still held her tight, feeling the need to protect her. Protect her from what? Himself? He tried not to think what might have happened *had* either of them been prepared.

He finally let go of her, but neither was able to make eye contact. He had sworn to himself to keep his hands off her; yet, every time she was near it proved impossible. He was a first-rate jerk, he realized. Not only had he let her father down, he'd let himself down. Where were his scruples?

Roxie was thoroughly mortified. How could she have let things get out of control? She wasn't dealing with some high school boy, she was deal-ing with a grown man. A very virile man, she reminded herself. No doubt he would remember this experience for years to come.

She was weary of the frustration she felt every time he called their lovemaking to a halt and was humiliated by her lack of experience, but most of all, she was tired of her roller-coaster emotions. One moment she wanted him as much as her next breath, but the next minute she felt unsure and incapable. Tyler made her deal with feelings she had somehow escaped until now.

"I think you should leave, Tyler," she said, trying to remain calm. Her insides churned with unvented need. She would rather appear rude than embar-rass herself further. "I have a lot of work to do, and you have to clean up so you can go to the restaurant."

Her words caught him by surprise. She was throwing him out. And there were so many things he wanted to say to her. He certainly didn't want her to feel like a freak because she was inexperienced. He stared at her a full minute, and she didn't flinch. "Okay," he finally said. "I'm on my way out." He pushed through the screen door and let it close behind him.

Roxie heard his footsteps on the stairs and was thankful he was gone. She stood there a while with her eyes closed, trying to get her emotions under control. She opened her eyes and glanced around the apartment, sighing heavily at all the work to be done. She welcomed it. Perhaps it would take her mind off Tyler and allow her to vent her frustration. She worked late into the night, scrubbing the wood floors until she was certain she had gotten off all of the old wax. When Lela dropped by later with a plate of food, she almost fainted from the smell of ammonia.

"Lord, girl, you need to open some more windows," the woman said, tears streaming down her face.

Although Roxie invited Lela to stay, she was thankful the woman declined. She knew Lela could smell trouble a mile away, and Roxie wasn't ready to try and explain the volatile relationship between Tyler and herself. She barely touched the food on her plate, then went back to work. It was after two in the morning when she took her bath, put clean sheets on the old feather mattress, and fell onto it. But sleep did not come easily. Every time she closed her eyes she saw Tyler's face.

The following day Roxie worked with the same vengeance. Tyler had obviously spent the night at the restaurant, because his car wasn't in the driveway when she awoke. She tried not to think how and with whom he had spent the evening. Instead she concentrated on getting as much done as she could before she started her job the next day.

Although she had scrubbed the floors to the bare wood, Roxie decided not to reapply wax until after she painted. She went over to the house and knocked on the back door. Lela answered it and frowned. "How come you're knocking on the door? Can't you open it by yourself?"

"I came for a can of paint."

Lela nodded. "Well, you know where Clem keeps everything, just help yourself. I'll pour us a cup of coffee and we can sit for a spell. You had breakfast yet?"

"I'm not hungry," Roxie yelled over her shoulder as she made her way through the dining room, into the hall, and up the stairs. She found all the paint in the bedroom Clem had worked in last. There were also enough drop cloths, paintbrushes, rollers, and paint trays to supply a small army of painters. Roxie took one of each and carried them downstairs.

When Roxie entered the kitchen, she saw Lela

had already prepared a plate of ham biscuits and had poured two cups of coffee. "Sit down and have a cup with me," the woman said. "Since you moved out back I don't have nobody to talk to. Mr. Sheridan's mood is so vile, I don't dare speak to him."

Roxie took the chair across from Lela, grateful for the cup of coffee. Lela convinced her to eat a couple of the biscuits and had just poured her a second cup of coffee, when Roxie heard Tyler's car pull up.

"I have to go," Roxie said, jumping out of the chair as though someone had slipped a thumbtack onto the seat. "Thanks for the coffee and biscuits," she mumbled, trying to get her supplies together. She said good-bye and hurried out the back door, and slammed right into Tyler as he came up the steps. He was wearing his black slacks and white shirt and carrying his dinner jacket over one arm. Her paint tray, brush, and roller tumbled to the ground.

"Hey, where's the fire, Red?" he asked, bending forward to pick up the strewn items. He stopped on his way up again to admire her legs in a pair of cutoffs. Her faded T-shirt stretched tightly across her breasts, making him ache for her in the worst way.

"I . . . uh . . . have a lot of work to do today," she said. How could the man look so calm after what had happened between them? she wondered. Unless, of course, something even more stimulating had taken place afterward.

"Here, let me carry this stuff up for you," he offered.

"No!" Roxie saw the look of surprise on his face. "I mean, you've done enough already."

He shrugged. "Whatever you say." He piled the items in her arms. "By the way, how did you sleep last night?"

"Why?"

Another shrug. "I just wanted to know how comfortable that old mattress was, that's all."

"Oh. Fine. I slept like a baby."

Damn, she'd done it; she'd made him think of her curled up all warm and cozy in the bed. "By the way . . ." He paused and reached into his shirt pocket. "I got a call from my mechanic this morning. He says your transmission is shot. You can reach him at this number."

Roxie took the slip of paper. "Thanks," she said, looking grim. No telling how much it was going to cost. She would have to call the man and tell him to park her car behind his garage until she came up with the money.

"Well, don't work too hard," he said. "Remember, you start your new job tomorrow. I've got a waitress waiting to train you. Can you be ready by three o'clock?" When Roxie nodded, he went on. "Bertie will help you find a uniform, then show you around the place and explain how we do things."

Roxie forced a smile. "I'll be ready."

Lela opened the back door. "You have a telephone call, Mr. Sheridan."

Roxie said good-bye and hurried away, carrying her load of supplies. Tyler stepped inside the kitchen and headed for the telephone. "Who is it?" he asked Lela.

"Somebody who calls himself Reverend Norris. That wouldn't happen to be Roxie's father, would it?"

Tyler felt his gut tighten in response. "Uh, he's just somebody I met a long time ago," he said, trying to avoid the question. "I'll take the call in the den," he added, and left the room.

Roxie was ready and waiting the following afternoon, dressed in one of her nicer dresses. She had pulled her hair back and tied it with a white ribbon. She was nervous about starting her new job, but she gave Tyler a bright smile when he opened the door and helped her into his car. Conversation was strained between them, and Roxie knew it was because of what had happened in her apartment two days before—what happened between them every time they were alone! If Tyler wanted to pretend there was nothing between them, fine, she thought. He obviously meant more to her than she meant to him.

If he ever made up his mind whether he wanted any kind of relationship with her, she would be prepared. No matter what the cost to her heart.

Tyler parked his Mercedes behind the restaurant, and they entered through the back door. A slender middle-aged waitress named Bertie Peters

was already there. She smiled at Roxie as Tyler
introduced them, then disappeared into his office.

"You've never done waitress work of any kind?"
Bertie asked, looking somewhat skeptical. When
Roxie shook her head, the woman smiled again
although this time her smile seemed somewhat
forced. "Well, then," she said, clasping her hands
together. "Let's get started. I'll show you where to
put your purse, then we'll find you a uniform."

Twenty minutes later Roxie stood before the
mirror in the ladies' rest room, wearing a black
uniform with a starched white bib apron that was
identical to the one Bertie wore. "I can't believe
I'm actually going through with this," she told the
other waitress. "I don't know the difference between a soup spoon and a salad fork."

Bertie laughed. "You'll learn. Now be sure to
pull your hair back again so it doesn't fall in your
face."

Roxie ran a brush through her hair, then pulled
it back with the ribbon and pinned it up into a
neat knot at the back of her neck. She plucked a
few wisps over her forehead and stared back at
her own reflection. Typical girl next door, she
thought. She sat in a chair next to Bertie and
opened a shoe box. The white, rubber-soled shoes
fit her to a T.

"It doesn't matter if they're a bit tight," Bertie
explained, "because they'll give with wear. But if
they feel the least bit too big, you'll get blisters."
She smiled. "Any way you look at it, your feet are

going to hurt something fierce by the time this night is over. Ready?"

"As ready as I'll ever be," Roxie said. Bertie showed her where to hang her dress.

Once Roxie put her clothes away, Bertie instructed her how to polish the silverware and check the tables to see that each was set correctly. The white tablecloths had to be crisp and spotless, and the gold cloth napkins folded just so, Bertie told her. Each wine and water goblet had to be checked for dust or water spots and wiped clean with cheesecloth. Afterward they wiped the seats of the leather chairs. Bertie, a divorcée, Roxie learned, talked nonstop about her four grown children and showed Roxie pictures of her two grandchildren.

Once they had completed most of their tasks, Bertie gave Roxie a quick tour of the place. The Southern Belle, Roxie discovered, could accommodate more than four hundred customers in its four dining rooms. The main dining room on the first floor, which at one time consisted of several different rooms, had been opened into one large area. It could seat up to two hundred and fifty people for live entertainment. The other dining rooms located upstairs were smaller, accommodating private parties of fifty to sixty people. A large service elevator, which Tyler had installed, transported the food up to the second floor.

Tyler employed seventeen waitresses, Bertie informed Roxie, as they made their way down the free-floating staircase. But when the place was filled, as it often was, even seventeen people didn't seem to be enough.

The other waitresses started coming in at around five-thirty, all dressed in their uniforms. They tucked their purses away, clocked in, and went about the business of preparing for the night's crowd. Roxie found there was a mountain of chores to do before the first customers arrived. Bertie made introductions, but Roxie was sure she would never remember all the names.

Roxie found it difficult to concentrate on her last-minute duties once the tuxedo-clad musicians sauntered onstage to tune their instruments. She was awed by all she saw. By six-thirty, the dining room started to fill with beautifully dressed men and women. Soft laughter rang out, and an air of expectancy pervaded the room. Roxie envied the women in their finery, some looking as though they'd stepped out of the pages of *Vogue*. Roxie, who was accustomed to fast-food restaurants, tried to imagine herself going to all that fuss and bother to get ready for dinner.

She spotted Tyler from across the dining room, and realized she'd been seeking him out since her arrival. He had changed into his dinner clothes. Tall and lean and impeccably dressed, Roxie was sure he set many women's hearts fluttering. His movements were fluid and graceful as he strolled through the dining room, but there was an underlying strength and self-confidence and maleness about him that made her long for him in a way that shocked her as much as it surprised her. She already knew what one glance, one smile could do to her.

"My, but doesn't the boss look nice tonight," Bertie said, as though reading Roxie's mind. "But then he always does. Every waitress in this place has had the hots for him at one time or another, but he doesn't fraternize with the help."

Before Roxie could respond, the hostess announced they had customers. "Just watch me," Bertie said, "and you'll pick up the routine in no time."

Roxie followed and listened as Bertie introduced herself to the two couples at the table. She took their drink orders, always remaining pleasant and professional. Roxie then followed Bertie to the bar, where the drink orders were filled quickly and efficiently by one of three bartenders. The men looked dashing in black slacks and vests, and white shirts with bow ties. Each carried a cigarette lighter and drew it immediately whenever a customer pulled out a cigarette. The staff at the Southern Belle were real pros.

Tyler listened politely to the pudgy woman who was speaking to him, but his mind was elsewhere. He had spotted Roxie several times but had not had a chance to talk with her. It probably was just as well, he thought. The other waitresses might start asking questions if he paid too much notice, and he didn't want to put Roxie on the spot. He took a sip of the frozen concoction one of the bartenders had made him, minus the alcohol. After having spent the first thirteen years of his life with alcoholic parents, Tyler never had acquired a taste for it. Nevertheless he'd learned long ago the best wines to select for his customers, and he stocked only the finest brandy.

The woman drifted away, and Tyler was thankful for the reprieve. He glanced around the dining room, pleased to see it was filled. Not bad for a Monday night, he decided.

He swelled with pride as he surveyed the room. The wallpaper he'd chosen for the main dining room was a white latticework with sprigs of ivy. White oscillating fans—at least a dozen of them—hung from the ceiling and turned slowly. Oversize flowerpots stood beside each doorway, filled with a variety of sweetly scented flowers. He'd achieved the effect he'd hoped for, of dining in a summer garden in a romantic setting in the South. And sometimes, when Curly Jones, the bandleader, played his slow and gentle version of "Dixie" on his trumpet, it caused a hush to fall over the room. Curly never failed to touch his audience. All that considered, Tyler knew the restaurant had succeeded beyond his wildest dreams. At the age of thirty-three he was called the boy wonder of the restaurant world.

At times Tyler marveled at his success. It had not come overnight, nor would it have come at all had it not been for the man who'd practically raised him and taught him the restaurant business. The same man who'd left Tyler everything upon his death, including his modest but popular restaurant. Tyler had sold the place for a considerable sum. Although he'd never once accepted a paycheck from Therman Lewis, his benefactor, he had saved almost every penny he'd made in tips over the years. That money, along with what he'd gotten from the sale of the restaurant, had made a sizable down payment on the mansion he bought for his own restaurant.

Although the place had needed major repairs and restoration work when Tyler had first seen it, it was unlike anything he'd ever laid eyes on in his life, and a far cry from the rundown house where he'd lived with his parents. The view from the veranda was breathtaking, and on a clear day he could gaze across the harbor at Fort Sumter, where the first shots had been fired in the Civil War. His customers enjoyed sitting on that veranda, sipping mint juleps. Not only was it romantic, it was a gentle reminder of life in the Old South.

The Southern Belle Supper Club was the result of years of struggle. Within its walls, he almost could lock out his ugly past. But sometimes, when he let the memories in, he could recall the sounds inside his head as a big fist came down on him— his father's fist. He could hear the echo of his ears ringing from the very impact. Tyler closed his eyes for a second, and when he opened them, he found himself once again within the protective walls of the Southern Belle.

The Southern Belle was his mistress; he lavished attention upon her unstintingly. She was his child; he nurtured her unselfishly. Yet, something was lacking in his life.

In two hours time Roxie Norris wished she'd never heard of the Southern Belle Supper Club. Just following Bertie through the large dining room, the hallway, and back and forth to the bar was enough to give her a bad case of fallen arches. Customers filled the tables, all demanding to be pampered. Roxie was hot and thirsty, and her feet ached from her new shoes. Sweat streamed down her neck and back. She was never going to make it through the night!

Together she and Bertie pushed an enormous metal cart filled with a large order out of the kitchen and into the dining room. They had just pulled it up to the table of businessmen who were eagerly awaiting their meal when Bertie was summoned to another table.

"Do you think you can set these platters out?" she asked Roxie.

Roxie glanced at the serving cart. All ten men had ordered big T-bone steaks. All she had to do was clear away their salad bowls and figure out how each man had ordered his steak cooked. It should be simple, she told herself, since Bertie had arranged them on the cart in order. "Sure," she said confidently. "I can do it. You go ahead." Bertie hurried away.

Humming to the band music, Roxie began clearing away salad bowls, dressings, and cracker baskets, while at the same time passing out platters of steak. Easy as falling out of a tree, she thought. Then, much to her consternation, she found she was short one T-bone. She fumbled through the debris that she'd tossed on the cart, but couldn't find it. It was no wonder, she told herself. The dining room was so dark she couldn't see her feet in front of her. The only light came from the bandstand and the candles on the tables.

Roxie quickly explained the situation to the man and pushed the cart hurriedly in the direction of the kitchen. Several salad bowls tumbled to the floor, lettuce and salad dressing spilling onto the carpet, but she didn't have time to worry about that. She grabbed the bowls and tossed them back onto the cart.

It took Roxie several minutes to explain her problem to the cook, who was too busy to listen. "You asked for ten T-bone steaks and I gave you ten T-bone steaks," he said.

Roxie sighed and decided to go check her cart once more, but when she reached the dishwasher, she found her cart had already been unloaded. There was no steak, no salad bowls—nothing. "Damn!" she muttered to herself, searching for the man she'd seen unloading the carts earlier and stacking the dishes into the dishwasher. Perhaps he'd seen the steak. She called out to him, stepping carefully across the wet, slippery floor, but the kitchen was so noisy she was certain he couldn't hear her. She made her way around the long metal counter toward a room where more dishes were stored. She gasped when she found the man sitting on a crate, eating her T-bone steak.

"Stop!" she yelled, motioning wildly at the plate. The man, obviously frightened out of his wits, jumped, sending the platter crashing to the floor. Roxie retrieved the partially eaten steak and moaned aloud. Too late. Half the meat was gone. Perhaps if she covered it with a bit of parsley . . .

"What's going on?" Bertie asked, coming up behind Roxie. "One of the guys at our table is complaining about not having a steak." She saw the piece of meat in Roxie's hand and wrinkled her nose.

"Who's complaining?" Both women glanced up in surprise to find Tyler Sheridan standing nearby.

Roxie had the sudden urge to climb into the gigantic garbage disposal and end it all, but unfortunately she owed it to Bertie to explain what she'd done. "It's all my fault," she confessed, and tried to explain the mixup. "The steak must've been on the bottom shelf of the cart, beneath the pile of salad bowls," she added. "By the time I found it, it was too late." She held up the piece of meat as evidence.

"Order the man another steak," Tyler told Bertie. "And give him a fresh drink while he waits. Tell him there's no charge for his dinner this evening." Bertie nodded once and hurried over to the cook.

Roxie handed the piece of meat back to the man who ran the dishwasher. Suddenly he didn't seem

America's most popular, most compelling romance novels...

Here, at last...love stories that really involve you! Fresh, finely crafted novels with story lines so believable you'll feel you're actually living them! Characters you can relate to...exciting places to visit...unexpected plot twists...all in all, exciting romances that satisfy your mind and delight your heart.

EXAMINE 6 LOVESWEPT NOVELS FOR

15 Days FREE!

To introduce you to this fabulous service, you'll get six brand-new Loveswept releases not yet in the bookstores. These six exciting new titles are yours to examine for 15 days without obligation to buy. Keep them if you wish for just $12.50 plus postage and handling and any applicable sales tax. Offer available in U.S.A. only.

☐ **YES,** please send me six new romances for a 15-day FREE examination. If I keep them, I will pay just $12.50 (that's six books for the price of five) plus postage and handling and any applicable sales tax and you will enter my name on your preferred customer list to receive all six new Loveswept novels published each month *before* they are released to the bookstores—always on the same 15-day free examination basis.

40311

Name_____

Address_____

City_____

State_____ Zip_____

My Guarantee: I am never required to buy any shipment unless I wish. I may preview each shipment for 15 days. If I don't want it, I simply return the shipment within 15 days and owe nothing for it.

R9234

Get one full-length Loveswept FREE every month!
Now you can be sure you'll never, ever miss a single
Loveswept title by enrolling in our special reader's home
delivery service. A service that will bring you all six new
Loveswept romances each month for the price of five—and
deliver them to you before they appear in the bookstores!

Examine 6 Loveswept Novels for

15 days FREE!

(SEE OTHER SIDE FOR DETAILS)

to be hungry, and he merely tossed the meat into the disposal. She was embarrassed to meet Tyler's gaze. "I'm sorry," she muttered. "I'll be more than happy to pay for the steak."

Tyler reached out and squeezed her hand affectionately, hoping it went unnoticed by the others. "It's okay, Red. I can afford to lose one T-bone dinner. Not every night, mind you." He let go of her hand and made his way out of the kitchen.

Roxie stood for a moment feeling like an idiot. Then she ventured back into the fray.

Six

Because it was Monday night, the slowest night of the week, the waitresses got out earlier than usual. Roxie had taken off her shoes as soon as she'd gotten in the car and planned to soak her aching feet the minute she got home. Tyler was unusually quiet during the drive, but Roxie thought it was just as well. They seemed to embarrass themselves every time they were alone together.

It was shortly after midnight when Tyler pulled into his driveway, and Roxie was relieved to say good night and climb the stairs to her apartment.

Roxie unlocked her door and flipped on the light switch, then kicked off her shoes once more. She hurried into the bedroom, slipped off her uniform, and donned her cotton robe. She found an old washtub beneath the kitchen sink and filled it with hot tap water. She set the tub carefully on the floor beside the kitchen table and sat down, then tested the water with her toes. Several minutes passed before she was able to submerge both feet into the steaming water, but when she did, she closed her eyes and sighed. It felt wonderful.

Roxie had worked hard that night, and she was proud of herself. She'd been in town only a few days and had an apartment and a job that would see her through until her new job started in the fall. What made her most proud was the way people accepted her for who she was—not Reverend Norris's little girl any longer and the youngest of his eight children. Her father would not overshadow her life as he had in Summerville.

Her father hadn't always been overprotective of her, she admitted to herself. Only after her mother's death a little over three years ago had she started to feel as if he were smothering her. Even when she had moved into her own apartment shortly afterward, her father had found excuses to drop by often. She escorted him to all church and social functions, when, sadly enough, a number of nice widows gladly would have gone in her place. Perhaps with her out of the way, her father would try to rebuild his life and give her a chance to build one of her own.

A knock at the door startled her and her eyes popped open. "Who is it?" she asked loudly, wondering if Lela had waited up for her.

The door opened a crack and Tyler called out. "It's me. Don't you know better than to leave your door unlocked at this time of night?"

The man was worse than her father, she thought. "Is that why you stopped by? Just to make sure I was locked in safely for the night?" She heard the door close, then footsteps approached the kitchen.

Tyler came into the room and smiled when he saw what she was doing. "I suspected as much," he said, walking over to her chair. "That's why I brought this." He held up a box of Epsom salts.

"Thank you," she said, warmed by his thoughtfulness. But as usual, it was the man himself who captured her attention. He was dressed in his form-fitting black slacks and white shirt. He had removed the bow tie and unbuttoned the collar of his shirt so that it fell open and revealed several sprigs of black chest hair. She watched him as he poured a generous amount of the salts into the hot water.

"Keep it," he told her, setting the box on the table and giving her a knowing look. "You're going to need it until you break in those shoes."

Roxie smiled. Sometimes he really could be nice. Especially when he wasn't trying to treat her like a five-year-old or kiss her senseless. "Sit down," she said, indicating the chair beside her. "Would you like a soft drink? Lela picked up a few groceries for me when she went to town."

He shook his head. "I just had a glass of iced tea."

"Oh." She nodded. Conversation seemed to drop off at that point, and she felt uncomfortable. "Bertie was very sweet tonight, showing me around and all. I really like her."

"I'm glad."

"I'm sorry about the steak."

"Forget it."

"And the dishes I broke when that tray slipped out of my hand."

"You'll learn."

It was quiet again. "You must be very proud of the Southern Belle," she said. "It's the most beautiful restaurant I've ever seen. What made you decide to go into the restaurant business in the first place?"

He shrugged. "A man I lived with for a long time taught me the business." Tyler studied her for a moment. "You don't know very much about me, my . . . uh . . . background, do you?"

"Only that my father has a high opinion of you. Why do you ask?"

Tyler leaned back in the chair and crossed his legs at his ankles. His slacks tightened across his thighs, and Roxie's gaze followed the masculine line from his knees to his hips, silently giving her feminine approval. "Your father sort of saved my life."

"Oh?" She raised her eyes to his.

Tyler saw she was truly interested but wondered if he should tell her anything about his life before moving to Charleston. There were a lot of things he had wanted to forget over the years, things he blamed on youth and ignorance. "I didn't have the kind of life you had growing up, Roxie," he said, then smiled. "I remember when I stayed with your family, I kept comparing it to the Andersons on *Father Knows Best*."

Roxie laughed. "You obviously don't know what it's like to live in a house with one bathroom and be the youngest of eight children." She saw her comment had amused him, and she felt more comfortable. After watching him mingle with Charleston's elite at the Southern Belle she thought he seemed different somehow. She wondered how many sides there were to Tyler Sheridan. She had watched him dance and charm women all evening, and she couldn't help wondering if perhaps one of them was special to him.

"What are you thinking about?" he asked, noticing the way her brow had creased into a frown.

"Huh?" Roxie was interrupted from her thoughts. "Oh, I don't know," she said. She wasn't about to confess her feelings. "A lot of things, I guess. Like where your parents are," she said, trying to get onto a safe topic. "Do they still live in Summerville?"

Tyler glanced away, and for the first time he noticed she had painted the kitchen. But, then, he realized, when he was around her, he noticed very little except how she made him feel. "My parents moved away from Summerville a long time ago. As for where they are . . ." He paused and shrugged. "I haven't the slightest idea."

"Doesn't that bother you?" she asked?

"I really don't give a damn." He saw that his reply shocked her. He stood and shoved his hands in his pockets and walked over to the sink with his back to her. "You don't know how it was, Roxie. And I don't think I could make you understand. I didn't live in one of those prim little houses near the Baptist college. I lived in another section of town that you're probably not familiar with."

"So? I was taught a long time ago that material things weren't important."

He laughed and turned around to face her. "Oh, Roxie," he said, giving her a patronizing smile. He didn't want to tell her about the ugly things in his life especially since she seemed to have had such a sheltered upbringing.

"You know, it really irks the daylights out of me when you talk to me like that. As if I can't comprehend things," she said hotly. "I wasn't raised in a plastic bubble, Tyler. I can deal with the realities of life."

"Okay, you want to know about my life," he said matter-of-factly. "What would you like to know? About my parents? Okay, they were alcoholics. No, let's get down to the nitty-gritty." For some reason he felt angry. "They were drunks, pure and simple. When they drank, they fought. My old man put my mother in the hospital more times than I can remember. And when he wasn't beating her, he was beating me. Do you get the picture now?"

"I get the picture. And I haven't crumbled into little pieces." Inside, though, she felt sorry for the boy who had endured it, but she knew pity would only fan his anger. "So then what?" she asked, feeling the need to challenge him. That was the only way she was going to learn something about him.

"Then I guess I sort of went crazy or rebelled, I don't know. I had been ripping my old man off for years. He'd get drunk and pass out, and I'd rob him blind. He blamed my mother, but I didn't care. Then I guess I got mixed up with the wrong crowd. By the time I was ten I was stealing hubcaps. By the time I was thirteen I was breaking and entering."

"Did you ever get caught?"

"Yeah, I got caught," he said grimly.

"I'm glad you don't have to live like that anymore."

He pondered the thought. "I guess I was lucky enough to find someone who believed I was special." He paused. "You see, when you've been beaten all your life, you don't have a high opinion of yourself. You lose your self-confidence, your self-esteem. Your father gave it all back to me, as did the man he sent me to live with." The smile he gave her was almost boyish. "And so did you," he added.

"Me? What could I have done? I was only four or five years old at the time."

"You followed me everywhere I went, begging me to play ball with you. You said I was the bestest person in the world. Believe it or not, those words

stuck with me. I wanted to be the best I could be."
He paused and glanced down at her feet soaking
in the bucket. "Ever had a foot rub?"

The question took her by surprise. "No-no." She
had a feeling he was changing the subject on
purpose. "And I don't want one," she said truthfully.

"Well, that's too bad, because you're about to
get one." He grinned devilishly as he left his chair
and knelt before her, then reached into the bucket
of water and brought up one slippery foot. She
tried to pull free, but he only grasped it tighter.
"Anybody ever tell you that you've got cute toes? A
little tense maybe, but I'll take care of that. Let's
see, how does that game go? This little piggy went
to market—"

Roxie blushed to the roots of her hair. "Tyler, I
really don't want a foot rub. Besides, you're going
to get your shirt wet."

"To hell with my shirt. Now would you sit still
and shut up?" She shook her head, realizing the
situation was hopeless.

"That's better."

Roxie gripped the edge of her chair for support
as he began to caress her foot with his hands. Her
robe fell open at her thighs, and she let go of the
chair long enough to pull it closed. She wasn't
sure whether it was his touch that was stealing
her breath away or the fact that his shirt gaped
wide enough for her to see part of his broad chest.
Perhaps it was his hands. Feathered with black

hair they were a vivid contrast to her fair skin. They were masculine hands, but she knew only too well how gentle and coaxing they could be. How could a foot rub be so sensual and erotic? she asked herself, feeling her pulse race. "I think that's enough," she said quickly.

"You're right. It's time I did the other foot."

He ignored her protests. When her toes accidently brushed the crotch of his slacks, Roxie felt heat rush to her cheeks. Although he didn't say anything, one corner of his mouth turned upward, letting her know the encounter hadn't gone unnoticed. He continued drawing circles with his thumbs along the very center of her sole, until Roxie's entire leg tingled.

"Now, doesn't that feel good?" he asked.

The timbre of his voice and the hypnotic motions of his thumb made her light-headed. She felt as though she were turning to putty. Lord, what power did the man have over her that he could turn her insides to mush every time he touched her? "Tyler?" Her voice was a croak.

"Hmm?"

"I'm . . . uh . . . kind of tired."

"What color nail polish do you wear?"

"Huh? Oh, it's called Deep Coral, I think."

"Nice. Real nice," he added, aware his voice sounded strange. He was edgy—his nerves stretched tight like a rubber band. "Sit still while I get a towel," he said. He hurried out of the room.

Roxie stopped holding her breath and air rushed

from her lungs. Was Tyler trying to seduce her with a foot rub? No, surely not, she told herself. He was being thoughtful, considerate . . . while she was overreacting. It wasn't Tyler's fault she turned dreamy eyed and giddy every time he touched her.

Tyler jerked a towel from the rack in the bathroom, then leaned his head against the door frame. Perspiration beaded his upper lip. Why did he go bananas every time he was around Roxie? He certainly hadn't planned on getting so turned on by a foot rub, for heaven's sake! He'd used it as a diversionary tactic, to get off the subject of his past. Pull yourself together, he told himself. He took a deep breath and left the bathroom.

Roxie noticed the grim look on Tyler's face when he came back into the room. "Is anything wrong?" she asked.

"Everything is fine," he said, avoiding eye contact. He knelt before her and took one small foot between his hands and patted it dry with the worn towel. If only he could keep his eyes off those trim ankles, he thought—and the spot where her calves flared out gently then curved inward just under her knees. She had the most shapely legs he'd ever seen. He already knew how nice her thighs and hips were. He'd stared at them enough when she'd had on those indecent cutoffs that had set his blood on fire. He dried the other foot. It was so dainty and feminine, so tempting. A rush of desire caused the front of his slacks to tighten.

It was more than he could take.

Roxie's head snapped up when she felt Tyler's lips brush the inner sole of one foot. She was certain she was going to slide right off the chair and into his lap. She held her breath as his mouth inched past her ankle and calf and stopped at her knee. She gazed at him in outright astonishment. Her robe fell open at the knee, and she reached out to adjust it, but Tyler was faster. He slipped his hand inside the garment and caressed her thigh. Roxie was powerless to object. She sucked her breath in sharply as his lips moved past her knee and followed the path of his hand. His breath was hot against her skin. It seeped through the flimsy material of her panties, and she squirmed uncomfortably in her chair. Every kiss, every caress made her yearn for more.

White-hot desire shot through Tyler's loins as he inhaled the fragrance of Roxie's body. He wanted her. He wanted to take her there in the chair, teach her firsthand the pleasures his mouth and tongue ached to give. She filled him with a hunger he'd never known.

All at once Tyler swept her from the chair and into his arms. His passion-glazed eyes gazed into a pair of green, bewildered ones. When he entered her bedroom, he placed her gently on the bed. He kissed her deeply, his tongue tangling with hers. He opened her robe with eager fingers and discovered she wore only a lacy white bra and panties. He kissed her again, this time letting his hands roam freely over her body. He wanted her. He wanted her hot and wet and naked. His heart raced at the thought. Don't think, he told himself. Don't stop and think. He stroked her with deft fingers, knowing where he could evoke the most pleasure.

Roxie watched Tyler anxiously. Every caress brought her closer to the brink. His touch was light but sure, creating just enough pressure where her thighs met. She couldn't think straight, and he hadn't even removed a piece of his own clothing. Heaven help her. He was a master in the art of lovemaking, but then he'd probably had enough experience for four men. She, on the other hand, was inexperienced. She wanted to touch him, but she knew her efforts would seem clumsy at best. A more sophisticated woman would know exactly how to please him, she thought.

Tyler saw the look of uncertainty on Roxie's face and froze. Was she afraid? He blinked several times to clear his mind. What was he doing? How many times did he have to remind himself she was off-limits? In one fluid movement he was off the bed. He didn't see Roxie's questioning frown. He raked his hands through his hair, already muttering curses at his loss of control. Not only did she lack experience, she had made it plain she had no means of birth control.

Roxie suddenly felt very foolish. She pulled her robe together and tried to get a hold on her emotions. "What is it, Tyler?" she finally asked, tired of trying to figure out the man.

Tyler sighed. He turned around and was relieved to see she had covered herself. "Roxie, could we just forget it this time?" he asked. "Could we just this once try to pretend it never happened?"

Roxie saw the pleading look in his eyes and softened. "Yes, I suppose so," she said, a dull ache filling her heart. She desperately wanted some answers, but she knew he wasn't able to give them to her. "It's late," she said. "We're both exhausted. Would you mind locking the door on your way out?"

She was dismissing him. He nodded, relieved to be going. "G'night, then," he said hurriedly, already at the bedroom door.

"Good night." She was determined not to let him see how upset she was.

She didn't budge until she heard the door close behind him. She got up and readied herself for bed, feeling as though she needed a good cry to ease her frustration. She climbed into bed a few minutes later and stared at the ceiling. What could she have possibly done to scare Tyler? It had to be her fault. There seemed to be no other reason. She sighed heavily. She'd gotten herself into a fine mess, and her heart was going to pay the price.

She had fallen in love with Tyler Sheridan.

Roxie was assigned her own station two days later. "Stop looking so worried," Bertie said as Roxie paced the hall outside the dining room. "You'll do okay."

Roxie attempted to smile. Although she got along well with most of the waitresses, Bertie was her favorite. The two had become fast friends.

Roxie's first night went relatively well, yet not entirely without incident. She and Tyler discussed the events of the evening on the way home.

"I can't believe how angry that man got when I spilled au jus sauce on his slacks," she said. "I gave him five dollars to have them cleaned." She shook her head. "You can't please some people."

Neither had mentioned the scene in her apartment. It was a subject they both avoided, but it was never far from Roxie's mind.

Over the next couple of weeks Roxie's waitressing skills improved; at least she didn't have as many complaints. During the day she worked on decorating her apartment. Once she had a telephone installed, she called her father. "I'm sorry it took so long to call, Daddy," she said to the man on the other end of the line, "but I just had my phone installed today. Yes, I have plenty of money." She wasn't about to tell him she was saving every dime to have her car repaired or that she'd been robbed on her first day in town. After a lengthy conversation, Roxie hung up, feeling satisfied. Her father had sounded impressed that she'd found a job and an apartment so quickly.

When Roxie *was* finally able to have her car repaired, she was delighted. It cost her almost everything she had, but she knew she could make it up soon with her tips.

Everything was going well. Her only problem concerned Tyler. Perhaps it was her imagination, but he seemed to be avoiding her. Each time she entered the bar area for a cocktail, he pretended not to notice her, although he often sat at the head table conversing with friends and couldn't help but see her. Even as he chatted with customers, he watched the dining room closely, Roxie noticed, and saw most of what went on. Once or twice when Roxie had sought him out for a specific reason, he'd been polite to a fault but had remained businesslike.

Lela cornered her one afternoon. "Are you going to do something about it or do you plan to go on moping around for the rest of your life?" she asked as they were measuring the windows for curtains Roxie planned to make. Lela had coerced Tyler into carrying down the old-fashioned sewing machine from the attic and up the flight of stairs to Roxie's apartment.

Roxie glanced up at Lela in surprise. "What?"

"You heard me," the woman said, pursing her lips, "and don't pretend you don't know what I'm talking about. I may look ignorant—"

"Is it that obvious?"

"You look like a lovesick calf, if you don't mind my saying so." Lela released the metal end of the tape measure and it snapped closed. "You know, if you keep this up you're going to make yourself ill. I have this cousin who had a friend who knew of a woman who *died* of a broken heart."

Roxie looked doubtful. "Nobody can die from a broken heart, Lela," she said, knowing Lela sometimes got carried away with her stories.

"Well, this woman did."

Roxie frowned. "How old was she?"

"Oh, she was almost eighty-two," Lela said.

Roxie rolled her eyes. "Oh, for heaven's sake, Lela. Did it ever occur to you the woman died of old age?"

"No. My cousin's friend said the woman was the picture of health—before she was jilted, that is. I think you should take this as fair warning."

"Well, I promise I won't die of a broken heart," Roxie mumbled. But she was certain if anybody had the power to break her heart it was Tyler Sheridan. She had been watching for his car to come home at night now that she was driving herself back and forth to work. There were many nights he didn't return until the wee hours of the morning, and some nights he didn't return at all. Roxie began to suffer from insomnia, lying awake at night wondering where he was.

"You know what I think you should do?" Lela said, once they'd finished measuring all the windows. "I think you should try a new look. I know this salon downtown—"

"What's wrong with the way I look?" Roxie asked, interrupting her.

"You look like a kid, that's what. If I didn't

know how old you were, I'd guess you were in high school. If you expect Mr. Sheridan to take a second glance, you'd better stop trying to look like a cheerleader. Know what I mean?" Lela didn't wait for a reply. "The cashier at the grocery store has a daughter who went to this salon, and she said—"

"Okay, I'll go," Roxie answered quickly, deciding anything was better than enduring another one of Lela's stories. "What's the name of the place?"

Lela told her the name of the salon and Roxie called Information and got the number, then dialed. "They said they can take me at one o'clock this afternoon," Roxie said, hanging up the phone and checking her wristwatch. "I hope it won't take long."

"Why don't I drive you?" Lela suggested. "You might get lost."

When they arrived at the salon, Roxie was escorted to a chair. A man named Peter was assigned to her, and he told her what hairstyle he thought would best suit her features. After he cut several inches off her thick mane, he layered it and styled it in a way that used her natural curl to an advantage. Her hair, which had always been one of her best assets, now fell in soft waves around her face. Then Roxie was passed into the capable hands of a sweetly scented cosmetologist who looked like a candidate for a *Glamour* magazine cover girl.

The woman experimented with several colors of eye shadow and lipstick, showing Roxie what colors would best complement her red hair and fair complexion. After what seemed hours, Roxie emerged from the shop, brushed, blushed, and glossed.

"You know, you don't look half bad," Lela said, scrutinizing her once they stepped out into the sunlight. "I bet your own family wouldn't recognize you."

Roxie was reeling from the shock over what her new look had cost her, not to mention the purchases she was carrying in a small designer bag. "Do you realize I just spent fifty-seven dollars on makeup and shampoo?"

"It was worth every penny," Lela told her. "Why, I had no idea your eyes were so pretty. And that hair . . ."

"Think he'll notice?"

"He'd be blind if he didn't."

Roxie's excitement over her appearance was short-lived. Although Bertie and several other waitresses said she looked great, it was Tyler's good opinion she wanted. She came face-to-face with him that evening. As she waited for him to approve a customer's personal check, she noticed he kept glancing up at her with a puzzled expression.

"What did you do to your . . . uh . .. hair?"

"I had it cut."

"I thought you looked different."

Different? Her heart sank. She had spent a great deal of money on herself, and all he could say was she looked *different*?

When Roxie arrived home that evening, she was too wound up to sleep. She decided to sew instead of going to bed, and wondering what Tyler was up to. She had already made curtains for the kitchen and was trying to finish a pair for the living room. Although the place would never be the Taj Mahal, Roxie was proud of what she'd accomplished in redecorating it. She had spent the first week painting the apartment in a light apricot shade. Lela had given her wax for the floors that made them shine. Together they had picked out muslin material to make curtains. The curtains were gathered at the top and pulled back on the side, each panel tied with a big bow. Still, it was a tedious job trying to make them on a sewing machine she was certain had come over on the *Mayflower*. Although Roxie knew she would have to move once her new job started, she hoped Tyler would be able to rent the apartment once she left. At least her efforts wouldn't be wasted.

After having worked more than an hour, Roxie decided to make a cup of hot tea. She had just put the water on to boil when she heard a knock at the door. She stood rooted by the stove. It couldn't be Lela, because she knew the woman was always in bed by ten, and it was after two in the morning. She took a deep breath and walked to the door, cautiously unlocked it, and opened it a crack to find Tyler standing on the other side.

"I see you're locking your door these days," he said, nodding his approval.

"Is that why you came by? To make sure I had locked out all the perverts?" she asked coolly. How dare he ignore her for weeks, not to mention keep her up most nights, then show up on her doorstep at two in the morning as if it were the natural thing to do. She was further irritated by the smile her words evoked.

"No, actually, I saw your lights on and wondered if everything was okay."

"Just dandy."

"I see I've caught you at a bad time. Are you gnashing your teeth for any particular reason?"

Oh, the nerve of the man! Roxie almost choked on her anger. Before she could say anything, though, she heard water spitting onto the burner of the stove and ran into the kitchen, grabbing the pan by the handle. Boiling water sloshed over the side of the pan and burned her hand. "Ouch!" she cried, setting the pan quickly onto a cold burner.

Tyler was beside her instantly. "Here, run it under cold water," he said, taking her by the wrist and pulling her toward the sink. He turned on the faucet and held her hand under the running water. "That better?" She nodded. He grinned. "What would you do without me?"

Sleep nights, she thought to herself. "It's not

hurting anymore," she said, trying to retrieve her wrist. The smell of his after-shave had suddenly taken her mind off the burn on her hand.

"Want me to kiss it and make it better?" he asked, giving her a devilish grin that made her mouth go dry.

"No, what I'd really like for you to do is leave," she said.

Tyler frowned. "What's up, Red? Have I done something to make you angry?"

She didn't like the searching look in his eyes. She was afraid he might see too much. How could she possibly explain the way she felt without appearing a fool? What business was it of hers if he stayed out all night? She certainly had no claim on him. "I'm sorry," she said, refusing to meet his gaze. "I was just about to make a cup of tea. Would you like some?"

"Only if you'll go sit down on the sofa and let me make it for you. You've been on your feet all night." He shooed her out of the kitchen, and Roxie could hear him rummaging through the cabinets. He called out after a moment. "Cream and sugar?"

"Yes, please." Roxie made herself comfortable on the couch, and checked to make sure her cotton robe was buttoned all the way down.

Tyler joined her several minutes later carrying two cups of hot tea. He set one before her, and she thanked him. "So, how did it go tonight?" he asked, taking a tentative sip of the tea.

"Okay, I guess. I made it through the evening without spilling a drink or dumping a dinner on anybody. But I can't seem to get the drinks straight. I can't tell the difference between a scotch and soda, and a bourbon and water." She rolled her eyes. "One lady ordered a Grasshopper, and I almost laughed. But then I figured it was some kind of delicacy like escargot or caviar. Lucky for me I ran into Bertie, and she told me it was an after-dinner drink."

Tyler couldn't help but smile. He liked her. It wasn't only the fact that she had the power to make him crazy at times, which was one reason he had backed off during the last couple of weeks, but he genuinely liked her. And he had missed being with her. His feelings toward her were confusing as hell, but he was sure he never would tire of wanting to be around her. "You know, Roxie," he said. "I always smile when I'm with you."

Roxie gazed at him from over the rim of her cup. Those were not exactly the words she wanted to hear from him. For now it seemed she was going to have to accept his friendship, and forget any thoughts of romance. Yet it was difficult when all she wanted him to do was take her in his arms.

"I've been meaning to tell you, you've done a heck of a job on this place," Tyler said, interrupting her musings. "I didn't think it was possible to turn this old place into a real home."

Roxie glanced around the living room with appreciation. "I'm happy with it," she confessed.

"Once I finish making curtains, I'll start decorating a bit."

"I don't want you to spend your hard-earned money fixing the place up," he said. "Get Lela to pick up whatever you need."

"I really don't think that's right, since I haven't started paying rent," Roxie said. "I asked you twice to come up with a figure by the first of July. Today is the fifth. I'm beginning to think you're procrastinating."

"You're the most stubborn woman I've ever met, you know that?" He smiled. "Well, I'd better get to bed. I suggest you do the same. And I'll get back to you on the subject of rent, okay?"

For once she wasn't going to argue with him. She walked him to the door and he leaned over and kissed her lightly on the nose. "G'night, Red."

Roxie watched him make his way down the stairs and sighed. She felt loneliness stealing over her, and she wanted to cry out his name and ask him to come back. But she wasn't about to start something only to have him back off at the last minute. And now he acted as though nothing existed between them except friendship. That's what hurt her most of all. She knew she never could be a mere friend to Tyler Sheridan.

Tyler decided to take a walk instead of going directly to bed. The night air was cool, and he needed time to clear his head after spending the past half hour with Roxie. He had used the past two weeks to cool off, but he realized he was just as attracted to her as he'd been when he first saw her having the screaming meemies in his driveway.

Of one thing he was fairly certain. Roxie Norris was as attracted to him as he was to her. He could feel it as surely as he felt his heart beating in his chest. He couldn't help but wonder if she had acted cool to him tonight because he'd spent so many nights away. If he did come home at night he usually ended up gazing across at her apartment, visualizing her sleeping in that old iron bed. At least at the Southern Belle he had fewer distractions. Sometimes he drove along the beach and parked and stared out at the ocean, wishing Roxie were with him. He realized he forgot to compliment her on her new hairstyle. She really had spruced herself up, and he wondered if she had done it for him. The thought that she might have pleased him.

He shoved his hands in his pockets and leaned against a giant oak, a smile teasing the firm lines of his lips. Was Roxie trying to get his attention? Lord, he hoped so. Not that she'd have to work at it. She already had his undivided attention.

But where did that leave them? In the fall she would be teaching at a college on the other side of town. Naturally she'd look for another place to live, which meant she would move out of the apartment and away from him. She would meet new friends, perhaps a man. The thought made him ache inside. He realized suddenly that he wanted her in his bed but he also wanted her in his life.

He had fallen in love with her!

It took several minutes for it all to sink in, and when it did, Tyler's lips pressed into a grim line. What was he thinking? Roxie's father had sent her to him for protection, not so he could become involved with her. Besides, their backgrounds were so diverse, he was certain their goals in life would be equally so. Roxie had been loved and cherished and protected by her family. He, on the other hand, had come from the gutter.

This was his chance to prove himself, not only to the minister but to Tyler Sheridan. He had to prove he was a man of honor. And an honorable man would not take advantage of a woman whose father had entrusted her to his care.

Seven

When Roxie was summoned to Tyler's office a week later, she was sure he was going to fire her for an accident that had occurred the night before. She found Tyler sitting at his desk looking very businesslike. He had not yet changed into his evening wear, but Roxie thought he looked just as handsome in faded jeans and a white short-sleeve knit shirt that emphasized his tan. He motioned her to take a seat, but she declined.

"I know why you called me in here," she said, ready to defend herself. She didn't notice the flash of surprise on his face. "But in all fairness you should hear my side of the story."

Tyler, who hadn't the slightest idea what she was talking about, merely shrugged. "Okay, let's have it."

Roxie took a deep breath. "First, someone loaded

the metal serving cart wrong. They stacked the saucers too high on the cart, but I didn't realize it because I was so rushed. As I pushed the cart out the kitchen door, a busboy charged in from the other side, and whamo!"

"Whamo?"

"At least half the saucers crashed onto the kitchen floor and . . . well, I'm sure you know the rest." Even the hostess had come running to see what the commotion was all about.

Tyler winced mentally. "How many saucers would you say actually broke?"

She sighed and fidgeted with her hands. "Dozens." She paused. "I want you to know, I wasn't being negligent, that's all. I'm perfectly willing to hand over my paycheck for the duration of my employment and live on my tips. But I wouldn't blame you if you fired me."

Tyler was silent for a moment. Fire her? How tempting. Then he'd be able to think straight again. His gaze wouldn't constantly roam the dining room searching for her. But then, of course, he couldn't fire her. Not only because he owed it to her father, but because he'd be miserable without her. "Fire you?" he said, as though the thought had never crossed his mind. "I have no intention of firing you, Roxie. And this is the first I heard of the . . . accident. I was in my office most of the night discussing business."

"I thought you knew. I thought *everybody* knew. It certainly drew a crowd." She had to stop to catch her breath. "If you're not planning to fire me, why did you call me in here?" she asked, wishing she'd never mentioned the broken saucers. She was thankful she hadn't brought up the little accident she'd had with the gallon container of Thousand Island dressing.

"I want to offer you a job," he said simply. "My cashier quit this morning without notice. I wondered if you would be interested. You won't make as much as you do in tips, but I'll see you're paid well." He paused briefly so she could think over the offer. "Unless you'd rather keep your present position," he added, hoping she wouldn't put him out of business in the meantime.

Roxie pondered the suggestion out loud. "I would probably make a better cashier than a waitress." She laughed. "I can think of a dozen women who'd make a better waitress than me."

He could think of two dozen, but that wasn't the issue. "There would be other duties," he said. "You'd be responsible for closing out the register every night, but we would work closely together, and I would train you."

Roxie's interest perked. Work closely together? "Uh . . . when would you want me to start?"

"Preferably this evening. I'll be right beside you, so you don't have to worry about a thing. What do you say?"

She smiled. "I'll take it."

Tyler almost sighed his relief. The quicker he got her out of that waitress uniform the better.

· · ·

Had Roxie had any idea just how closely she would work with Tyler, she would have turned down the job. He rooted himself beside her and watched her every move. When they were alone, she turned to him. "I'm perfectly capable of handling a cash register," she told him bluntly. "You don't have to stand over me like a nursemaid."

"I want to be here if you need me," he replied.

"Well, you're making me nervous by looking over my shoulder every time I do something."

Her comment didn't deter him, because he stayed right beside her for the rest of the night. She constantly was aware of him, the smell of his after-shave, the timbre of his voice when he spoke to departing customers. The hair on her neck prickled each time he came up behind her. She felt like a kitten stuck in a tree, and she was thankful when the last customer had paid his bill and left.

"Now I'll show you how to close the register," Tyler said, once the restaurant had closed for the evening. The busboys were cleaning off tables, then piling chairs on them for the floor cleaning crew, the waitresses helping them. Tyler first had Roxie add up the receipts on an adding machine, then count the cash and charges to make sure the amounts matched. He put the money in a leather pouch and locked it in the safe behind his desk.

"You did very well," he said once they had completed the tasks. She was a much better cashier than waitress. It was obvious she was more at home in her new job.

"Thank you," she said. "Perhaps tomorrow night you won't feel inclined to glue yourself to my side."

Tyler chuckled. "Maybe I like being glued to your side," he said, a teasing lilt in his voice. "Have you considered that possibility?" He walked away before she had time to reply.

Over the next couple of weeks, Roxie became more adept at her job and began taking on more responsibility. Tyler didn't complain; in fact, it took some of the load off him. But the day he learned Roxie had placed an order with the meat salesman in his absence, he hit the ceiling.

"I've always ordered the meat," he said. "You don't know what we order or how much."

"You're right," she told him matter-of-factly. "That's why I pulled the last few invoices. So I could get an idea."

"And where did you find them?"

"In the filing cabinet in your office."

"You went through the filing cabinet in my office in my absence?" he asked, indignant.

"Was I not supposed to?"

"You could've asked."

"You weren't here."

"Next time, ask."

"Next time, be here."

They glared at each other, and for a moment, Tyler began to wonder who was in charge. Then it hit him. He hadn't had control over his emotions or his physical condition since he'd met the little redheaded brat-turned-woman. He stalked toward his office angrily. Just who the hell did she think she was?

Tyler was relieved when Roxie began calling her father once a week, it took the responsibility off his shoulders. As a result he felt less guilty and unconsciously started to think up excuses to show up on her doorstep.

"I need to check your plumbing," he said one Sunday afternoon. He cursed the fact that she was wearing her cutoffs. "I thought Baptist ministers frowned on that sort of dress," he said, indicating her short shorts.

"Lucky for me I'm not a Baptist minister, huh? Now what's this about my plumbing?"

He tried to look serious. Actually he was hoping she'd offer him a cup of tea, so he'd have a reason to stay. "Have you noticed any rust or corrosion on your pipes?"

"I haven't looked."

"You haven't looked?" he asked, as though it were a serious oversight on her part. "Well, this place is old. I got to thinking about it last night and decided I'd better check out the plumbing so you're not at risk." He couldn't help but notice how snug her shorts were, especially where her thighs met.

"At risk?" she repeated. "You sound like the warning label on a cigarette pack." He wore black denims, she observed. They were skintight. So tight in fact that she couldn't help but notice . . . She glanced away quickly. His yellow sports shirt fell open at the collar. Only a blind person could miss that curly black chest hair. Thank God she wasn't blind, she thought.

Tyler saw her lips curl at the corners. She obviously wasn't taking him seriously. He thought his excuse for coming over was rather clever. "You wouldn't want to take a chance on your pipes bursting and flooding the whole apartment." He tried to appear stern.

"You actually sat up last night and worried about that possibility? I would have guessed a Casanova like yourself—"

"Beg your pardon?"

"You haven't exactly been burning the home fires lately."

The smile he gave her was brazen. He stepped closer, so close she could see the light brown flecks in his eyes. "Oh, so you've been keeping tabs on me," he said in an incredibly sexy voice. "I'm flattered."

Roxie's mouth fell open in response. He mimicked her, then reached forward and pushed her jaw shut. She blushed. She literally could feel the heat bouncing off his body. Her own body reacted as always. Her breathing grew ragged and her nipples tightened in response. "Which . . . uh . . . pipes do you want to look at first?"

"The kitchen is a good place to start."

"The kitchen. Right. Would you like a cup of tea?" She led the way.

He followed. "I suppose I could find the time." He grinned secretly as he stuck his head in the cabinet beneath her sink. He moved some of the cleaning items out of the way and turned on his back in order to get a good view of the pipes. If only he knew even a little about plumbing, he thought. He found his gaze wandering elsewhere, however. From his vantage point, he had an excellent shot of her legs and derriere. "Not bad," he said aloud.

Roxie filled the kettle and tried to step over his long legs. "They look okay, then?" she asked, trying hard not to stare at his body from the chest down. But what was a woman supposed to do? she wondered. The man exuded maleness.

"They look great," Tyler said.

"I'm relieved to hear it," she answered, prying her gaze off him. She put the water on to boil.

"And so you should be. They look as though they'll hold out for a long time to come."

Roxie opened the refrigerator and reached for the milk. "You sound like an expert."

"I don't like to brag, but I consider myself somewhat knowledgeable on the subject."

"Sounds as if you chose the wrong profession. Ever thought of doing this for a living?"

"If I thought I could get paid for it." Tyler grinned as he caught a full back view of her behind. She had the cutest fanny he'd ever seen. Oh, Lord, she was bending over, he realized. He raised up to get a better view and banged his head on a pipe. He winced as pain shot through his skull.

"I have a cousin who's a plumber, and he makes very good money," Roxie said.

Tyler slid out from beneath the sink. "I'd better check the bathroom." He disappeared. Instead of checking the pipes, though, he picked up a bottle of her perfume. He smelled it and sighed. Yes, that was it, her special scent. When he returned to the kitchen, he looked satisfied. "Everything looks good," he said.

"I'm glad. I certainly wouldn't want you to lose any more sleep over it." She handed him a cup of tea.

Tyler set the tea on the counter and snaked his arms around her waist before she could reach for her cup. She yelped in surprise when he pulled her up against him. "Lady, if you had any idea how much sleep I *was* losing, you'd take pity on me and put me out of my misery."

Roxie didn't quite know what to say. She refused to meet his gaze until he crooked a finger under her jaw and raised her head so that she had no other choice.

"You like the way I feel against you, don't you?" he asked, sure that the temperature in the room had shot up ten degrees.

Roxie didn't answer. Instead she pushed away, trying to look as though she had been totally unaffected by the embrace. If Tyler Sheridan thought he could turn her on and off as if she were a light switch, he could think again. Still, her hands trembled violently and her pulse was doing double time.

Tyler merely smiled at the flushed face he'd learned to read so well. He could see her nipples beneath her lightweight blouse. She wasn't immune to him as she would have him believe. He took a sip of the tea and frowned, thinking how crazy he was for drinking it on such a hot day. But he'd drink boiling oil if it meant spending time with her. "So, would you like to go out tonight?" he asked, surprised by the words pouring out of his own mouth.

Roxie appeared equally surprised. "Go out? With you? On a date?"

"Well, it's not a real date," he said, hedging. "I've been invited to a cookout by some friends. They're nice people." Damn, he sounded as though he were asking her to the prom. But his brain seemed to work in reverse when he was with her, and holding her in his arms hadn't made it any better. He grinned to hide his nervousness. "Or, we could skip the cookout, go to a drive-in movie and neck." He laughed at the look she shot him. " 'Course, you probably haven't done much of that."

She gave him a coy smile. "Oh, I wouldn't be so sure," she said. "I've been around the corner before."

"You mean the block." he said, surprised.

"No, the corner. I've never made it around the entire block." Roxie couldn't contain her laughter as she said it. She was getting brazen in her old age. But it was worth watching Tyler's reaction.

Tyler didn't quite know what to say. "Well, do you want to go to the cookout?" he asked. He wasn't sure either of them could handle the drive-in.

"What time?"

"Six."

"I'll be ready."

Tyler left her apartment without drinking the tea, deciding he needed to take another walk. He had taken up jogging, something he despised, in order to work off his excess energy. His life had consisted of jogging and cold showers lately, he realized. Roxie Norris was changing right in front of him. First she had to go and get a new haircut. He couldn't get a lick of work out of his hired hands, especially Rusty, when she was around. And now she was deliberately taunting him!

Yes, she was doing it on purpose, the little witch. She not only made him aware of her at the Southern Belle, he often found her in his house visiting with Lela when he returned home after spending another miserable night on the couch in his office. Afterward her perfume hung in the air for hours, making him crazy.

She was pushing him past the breaking point. If he had any sense, he'd turn her little tush around and send her back to her father where she couldn't torture him anymore.

Instead he'd asked her for a date. Smart move, he told himself. Real smart.

Roxie was ready promptly at six. She wore white slacks and a navy and white cotton pullover. Tyler thought the outfit contrasted nicely with her light tan—one she'd got while gallivanting around the place half dressed, he noted sourly.

"You look nice," he said, holding the screen door open so she could lock her door.

"So do you." He wore khaki pants and a Christian Dior shirt. Together they walked down the stairs toward his car.

"You'll like Marge and Dave Preston," Tyler said, once they were on the main road. "Did I mention they have a new baby?"

"Really? How old?"

"Six or eight weeks."

"Shouldn't we take a gift?" Roxie asked.

He reached over and patted her hand. "I've already taken care of it."

The Prestons didn't live far and in no time Tyler pulled up beside the curb in front of their home, where several other cars were parked. Their host and hostess greeted them at the door. Several other couples introduced themselves, then Marge quietly led the women, including Roxie, into the nursery where the baby was sleeping.

"He's beautiful," Roxie whispered, gazing at the plump infant. She glanced up quickly. "It is a boy, isn't it?"

Marge smiled and nodded. "His name is David Junior, but we call him Davie."

The women each had a look at the tiny baby and then slipped quietly out of the room. Marge turned to Roxie. "I'll let you hold him later when he wakes up."

Dave had set up a bar on the patio and was in the process of taking drink orders when the women returned. Roxie, who had no idea what Tyler was drinking, asked for a glass of white wine.

Dave handed it to her. "I hear you're working at the Southern Belle," he said. "How long have you been there?"

"Almost eight weeks," Roxie said.

"Do you enjoy it?"

"Very much. The people are awfully nice."

Marge came up beside her and gave her a conspiratorial smile. "You're renting the apartment behind Tyler's house, I'm told. What's it like?"

"Oh, it's a very nice place. It wasn't at first, of course, but I've repainted it and made curtains—"

"Yes, but what's it like living behind Tyler?" Marge asked, grinning at the dark look Tyler shot her.

"It's okay," Roxie said. "I don't see him very much. He only comes by when he needs to check my plumbing."

Dave nudged Tyler in the ribs with his elbow. "In college we used to say etchings."

"David!" Marge gave him a playful smack on his arm. "Remember your manners."

"So what brings you to Charleston, Roxie?" a woman named Liz asked.

Roxie told her about the teaching position she'd start in the fall. Before she knew it, she found herself telling them all about her first day in town, how she'd been robbed by a couple of senior citizens, sprained her ankle, and ended up in the capable hands of Tyler's housekeeper, Lela. The group laughed and Roxie laughed with them. "It sounds funny now, but believe me, it was one of the worst days of my life."

Tyler frowned. It had been one of the *best* days of his life.

The couples chatted on while Dave cooked hamburgers on a gas grill and Marge served snacks. "I really like your friends, Tyler," Roxie whispered once she caught him alone. "Thanks for inviting me to come along."

"Thanks for coming." He looked down at her. Their gazes locked briefly, and Roxie felt her heart flutter. At times she wanted to tell Tyler exactly how she felt, but the words wouldn't come. It was as though something was standing between them.

Once the hamburgers were ready, everybody prepared their plates from a buffet table Marge had set up. Roxie sat next to Tyler on a picnic bench, conscious of his every move. His thigh pressed against hers beneath the table. He wasn't doing it on purpose, she told herself, but only because it was so crowded. She felt her pulse quicken every time his arm brushed hers or she caught the familiar scent of his after-shave. She wondered if her attraction to him was healthy. Her mind and body went topsy-turvy every time he was near. She knew it was a heck of a lot more than mere attraction that sent her into a tailspin every time he glanced at her. She had fallen head over heels in love with the man. What was she going to do about it? she wondered.

After dinner the men talked while the women chipped in and helped Marge clean up. When Marge heard the baby cry, she excused herself. Roxie and the others urged her to go ahead and nurse the child and leave the rest of the work to them.

When Marge returned some twenty minutes later, after having changed and nursed the baby, she held him out to Roxie, who was sitting in one of the chairs on the patio.

"Oh, my," Roxie said, gazing down at the plump little face. "He's absolutely beautiful." She held out a finger, and he grabbed it with his fist and refused to let go. "Look, he's smiling at me," Roxie announced proudly.

Dave shook his head. "Naw, it's just gas." Everyone laughed.

Roxie pressed her lips against the baby's head. "He smells so nice. Like baby powder." She glanced at Tyler and saw he was watching her closely.

Tyler looked away as soon as Roxie's gaze found his. Seeing her hold the baby made him feel things he had never felt before. He envied Dave for having such a wonderful family. Sometimes he regretted not having a wife and children of his own. His parents had shown him just how miserable family life could be if it went wrong, and he had never wanted to take the chance. But the thought of Roxie holding his child made his gut wrench with emotion.

"Okay, it's my turn now," Liz said, taking the baby from Roxie. The women took turns holding him as the two parents beamed proudly.

When it was time to leave, Roxie said her good-byes and thanked Marge and Dave for their hospitality. She was smiling when Tyler helped her into his car. "That was the sweetest baby," she said. "And so chubby," she added as Tyler steered the car out onto the main road. "I used to run the nursery at my father's church, and all the mothers accused me of spoiling their babies rotten."

"And did you?" he asked, glancing over at her.

"Yes, as a matter of fact, I did." They both laughed.

It was dark when they pulled into the driveway behind his house. He hurried around the car and helped her out. They looked at one another, both of them reluctant to say good night. "Want to come to my place for a cup of tea?" she asked.

He grinned. "I thought you'd never ask." He followed her up the stairs to her apartment, his eyes drinking in the swaying motion of her hips.

Once Roxie had prepared two cups of tea, she settled herself on the couch next to Tyler. "I really had a good time tonight," she said. "It must be difficult for you to get together with your friends, considering the time you spend at the restaurant."

Tyler shrugged. "I suppose."

"Why *do* you spend so much time there?"

"Because there's so much to do," he said. "Besides, I enjoy feeling needed, I guess."

She was surprised by his answer but realized he had just opened another door to his private self. "Everybody likes to feel needed," she said simply. "Look at Marge and Dave. They need each other. Their baby needs them." She paused and took a deep breath. "And I need you." There, she'd said it, and the ground hadn't swallowed her up.

Tyler was certain he had misunderstood her. "What?"

She smiled self-consciously. "You heard me." Roxie decided to lay her heart on the line. "I need you, Tyler, and I'd like to think you need me just a little." When he didn't answer, she went on. "I know your past was difficult and nothing like mine, but that doesn't matter. The future is all that matters."

Tyler sat frozen to his seat. "What are you trying to say, Roxie?"

She sighed. She had gone this far, she may as well go all the way. "Tyler, I'm in love with you," she said, meeting his gaze. "I have been for some time now. I wanted to tell you sooner but— "

"Don't say anything else, Roxie," he said, shushing her with a finger against her lips, as his heart turned somersaults in his chest. "You'll only end up regretting it later." He stood and strode toward the door. She followed.

"What do you mean I'll regret it?" she asked, her face a mask of confusion. "I know you care for me, Tyler. And you're a liar if you try to deny it."

Tyler's heart ached at the soft look in her eyes, the love that radiated from her face. He cursed her father, himself, and her for letting any of it happen. He longed to take her in his arms and tell her of his own love. He wanted to make love to her until he knew every inch of her body. And if he confessed his true feelings, he knew that was exactly what would result.

He would have to live with the guilt forever.

"I won't deny caring for you, Roxie," he finally said. "Of course I do." Her eyes lit up, and he hated himself for what he was about to say. "But I could never love you as a man *should* love a woman. I know you're all grown up now, but I still think of you as my old friend's little girl. I'm afraid that's how I'll always think of you." He saw the pain in her eyes and wanted to hold her and kiss it away. Her pain could be no worse than the emptiness he felt inside. When he spoke again, his voice was void of emotion. "If I've led you to believe otherwise, then I apologize."

Tyler turned away, no longer able to bear seeing the hurt expression on her face. "I'll let myself out," he said quietly. He opened the door, determined not to look back for fear that he'd lose the battle raging inside him. He closed the door behind him and made his way down the stairs.

He was angry. He wanted to pound his fists against something hard. Later he lay in his bed thinking. He hadn't changed one iota since he'd met Roxie Norris. He was the same shallow, empty man he'd always been. The only difference was that it had taken someone like Roxie to point it out.

His honor was intact, though, he reminded himself. He'd had the perfect opportunity to take her to bed, and he'd backed off. Honor. He wanted to laugh. Big damn deal.

Roxie pried herself off the sofa where she had been sitting for more than an hour. Tyler's words had literally turned her inside out. He may as well have taken a knife, stuck it in her heart, and twisted it.

Something wasn't right, she told herself. If Tyler truly thought of her in the terms he'd used, why then did he look at her as he did? Why had he taken her in his arms and kissed her senseless? Why had he told her he wanted her so badly it hurt?

Something was standing between them. How many times had he started to kiss her, only to stop as though he were afraid to touch her? Did it bother him that she was a virgin? Did he prefer more sophisticated women? A dozen questions popped into her head, and she knew she would spend another sleepless night trying to answer them.

Of one thing she was sure. She would keep her feelings to herself from now on.

Eight

Roxie and Tyler barely spoke to each other over the next few days. When they did, it concerned business. Although Roxie had been hurt by his rejection, the hurt quickly turned to anger. She wondered at first if she should move out of the apartment and find another job. Then she reminded herself she only had a few weeks left. It was almost the end of July. The restaurant would close for two weeks in mid-August, as it did every year, during which time it was cleaned, painted, and exterminated. And the entire staff would take their vacations, which Roxie was beginning to think they all needed.

Everyone was irritable. The chef was more demanding and less tolerant with the waitresses, slamming platters across the metal counter and hurling insults at those who were late picking up their orders. Accidents and arguments became the norm, until one evening Tyler himself stormed into the kitchen and insisted on peace. Although Roxie had no plans to go away on vacation, she knew she would welcome the reprieve. Bertie assured her they went through the same thing every year at this time.

"Will you be going to Summerville when the place closes?" Tyler asked Roxie one afternoon while she sat at his desk looking over the books— another duty she had taken on. Tyler had welcomed it because he hated bookkeeping.

Roxie shook her head. "No, I won't have time," she said, repeating what she had already told her father. He hadn't liked it one bit. She thought she saw relief in Tyler's eyes, but she was certain she had to be mistaken. "I have to go to the university for an orientation session. I need to pick up materials and prepare my lessons, which I should have started weeks ago." She saw him nod. "Also"—she paused and dropped her gaze—"I thought I'd use the opportunity to look for an apartment. "I just wanted to let you know in case you'd like to rent the place out in September."

Tyler didn't respond. Instead he shuffled through some of the papers on his desk and took a chair in front of it. Roxie went back to her work. "What's this?" he asked, holding up several insurance brochures.

Roxie glanced up. "Oh, I've been meaning to discuss the matter with you," she said. "I've checked into several insurance companies."

The fact that he hadn't authorized her to do so didn't surprise him. "And?"

"And I think we should drop the current plan."

"Any particular reason?" He thought the present plan was fine. He'd used the same company since he'd first opened the restaurant.

"It doesn't provide dental insurance. I can't tell you how many times I've heard the girls complaining about that. Most of them have children—"

"I can't afford to provide a dental plan," Tyler said, cutting her off. "Do you have any idea what it would cost?"

"As a matter of fact, yes. I have the figures in front of me." She handed him a slip of paper, and he frowned at the amount listed, just as she'd known he would. "There's a way to cut costs," she said, before he had time to object. "You already take a small percentage out of the waitresses' paychecks to cover some of the costs on the plan offered now. Suppose you could offer them a plan with a lower deductible, higher coverage on hospitalization, and a dental plan. You could divide the costs straight up the middle. It wouldn't cost you much more."

"You think they'd agree to have more taken out of their paychecks?" he asked.

She nodded. "The girls don't count on their paychecks to make a living. They count on tips. You know that as well as I do."

Tyler pondered the idea. "I don't know," he said, flipping through the other brochures.

"Why don't you leave it up to them to decide?"

Roxie suggested. "I could arrange for an agent to attend our next staff meeting and discuss the plan. Then you could outline the advantages and disadvantages. They could vote on it."

He tossed the brochures onto the desk and stood. "Okay, go ahead with it," he said, knowing she was right. The insurance plan he presently used didn't seem as comprehensive. If the employees were prepared to absorb some of the costs, why should he stand in the way? Still, his ego had made him react negatively. He thought he ran things pretty well. Now that Roxie had stepped in, she was intent on changing everything. Not that all her ideas were bad, he realized. He just didn't understand why she bothered. After all, she would be leaving in a couple of weeks. He frowned. He didn't like to think about it.

"Anything else?" he asked, before taking his leave.

"Just one thing," she said, closing the book she had been studying. "I think you should hire more busboys."

"What on earth for?"

Roxie stood, rounded the desk, and leaned against it. "Tyler, have you ever noticed what goes on around here every night when we close?"

"I think after almost ten years I pretty much know." He wondered if she had intentionally moved closer to throw him off guard.

"Then you realize that a lot of manual labor is expected from the waitresses?"

"What do you mean?"

"Once the customers are gone and the lights come on, the girls begin pulling tables apart and dragging chairs from under the tables."

"The busboys are supposed to do that."

"The busboys are busy trying to clean the tables and get the dishes to the dishwasher. In the meantime, the women do some of the heavy work, and there are a couple of them who simply can't lift."

"Okay." Tyler held his hands in the air. "Go ahead and hire as many busboys as we need. We'll offer the finest insurance plan and do what we can so the girls won't strain themselves. Never mind if I go broke in the meantime."

Roxie gave him a smug look. "C'mon, Tyler," she said. "I handle the books. You're making money hand over fist, if you'll pardon the cliché."

He glared at her. "Perhaps I let you take on more responsibility than I should have. Next you'll want to change the menu and redecorate the place."

"I considered it, but I won't be around long enough to see it through."

"Thank God for that." He stalked out of the room. Damn woman! he thought. She was driving him stark raving mad. Not only had she gained control of his mind and body, now she was taking over his restaurant. For the first time in his life, Tyler almost wished he drank.

When the big night finally arrived, everybody did an about-face. The girls were in a joyful mood, and even the cook stopped yelling. Everyone acted happy except Tyler. When Roxie hurried into his office in search of more ticket pads, he was waiting for her.

"I want to offer you a job," he said without preamble.

Roxie came to a screeching halt. "What?"

Tyler sat behind his desk looking very serious. "As my manager," he continued. "I never realized how badly I needed one until you came in and started taking some of the load off me."

Roxie suddenly became aware that her mouth was hanging open. She closed it. "I already have a job, remember? I'm a teacher."

"You teach business management. You'd be the perfect candidate for this job."

Roxie was still trying to overcome her shock. "I appreciate the offer, Tyler, but—"

"I'll top whatever they've offered to pay you," he cut in. He tried not to notice how tempting she looked in a silky rose-colored dress. Her long hair was braided and coiled at the nape of her neck. She had placed several sprigs of baby's breath neatly in the coil, which added a dressy touch to her appearance. He had wondered for weeks what she'd look like naked with that red hair hanging down her back.

Roxie didn't quite know what to say. "Tyler, the money isn't important. It just wouldn't work out." She knew darn well it wouldn't work. She had literally counted the hours until she'd be free of the Southern Belle and Tyler. The tension between them was unbearable. She knew in her heart she loved him, but she had accepted the fact that nothing would come of it. The sooner she got away from him, the quicker she'd get over it. She hoped.

Tyler stood, his gaze never leaving her face. He closed the distance between them with a slow but powerful stride. "I need you here," he said.

Had he said he needed her, she would have thrown her arms around his neck. What he needed, she thought, were just her skills, nothing more.

"I suggest you hire a manager, Tyler," she said coolly. "I'm finished here after tonight." She saw the pained expression on his face and her heart ached. But if only he knew how much pain she'd been in during the past few weeks. She turned on her heel and walked out.

A capacity crowd filled the Southern Belle on the last night before vacation and Roxie was kept busy. When the girls got behind, she stepped in, emptying ashtrays, taking drink orders, or whatever else was needed. Once the customers began leaving, she took her place at the cash register and didn't move until the last person had paid. It was well after midnight when the restaurant finally was empty.

Roxie sighed wearily once she'd closed out the register. She carried the money pouch into Tyler's office to the safe and found him gone. After checking with several people she learned he'd left more than an hour before. That meant she would have to stay and lock up.

The waitresses, many of them obviously feeling their vacation had already begun, ordered a big tray of margaritas. They sipped their drinks leisurely, while the new busboys stacked tables and chairs on the dance floor; the carpets would be shampooed the following week. Even the chef ventured out of the kitchen and had a beer, then chatted with a bartender amicably before returning to the kitchen.

Roxie passed out the paychecks, taking a minute to say good-bye to each girl. She'd become friends with most of them and knew she'd miss each one. Especially Bertie. She handed Bertie her check and hugged her.

"Don't start that sentimental stuff," Bertie said. "My husband used to pull that every time I kicked him out. It took me twenty-seven years to get rid of him."

Roxie laughed. "I'm going to miss you, Bertie."

"Hey, not so fast, kid," the woman replied. "We're all going out to breakfast. Why don't you join us?"

Roxie nodded. "Thanks, I will."

As soon as they'd all clocked out and located their purses, the girls piled into their cars and drove to an all-night restaurant close to the Southern Belle. Once inside they began pulling tables together, much to the obvious surprise of the owner.

"How about putting on a couple of fresh pots of coffee," Bertie told the man. "You're going to need them to serve this group."

The girls chatted over breakfast, each one promising to visit the other before they returned to work at the end of the month. As Roxie paid her check, she glanced at her watch in disbelief. They'd spent two hours in the place. It was after three o'clock in the morning.

"Listen," Bertie said, pulling her aside. "I live only a mile from here. Why don't you spend the night at my place instead of driving home alone?" Bertie knew Roxie lived in the apartment behind Tyler's house. "I certainly wouldn't want to drive on those country roads at this hour of the morning. What if your car broke down?"

"Are you sure you have room?" Roxie asked, knowing anything was possible with her car. Despite her problems with Tyler, they usually left together each night so he could follow her home, and the thought of going home to her empty apartment didn't hold any appeal.

"Of course I have room," Bertie assured her.

Roxie followed Bertie's car and parked in front of a modest brick house. Inside pictures of Bertie's children and grandchildren filled every nook and cranny. Roxie was dead on her feet. Bertie, who looked equally tired, tossed her a nightgown and pointed her in the direction of the guest room.

"I have an extra toothbrush in the medicine cabinet in the bathroom," the older woman said, trying to stifle a yawn. "I bought it three years ago just in case I ran into the man of my dreams and decided to bring him home with me." She rolled her eyes. "You'll notice it's still in the package it came in." They exchanged tired smiles.

Roxie changed into the nightgown, washed her face and brushed her teeth, and fell into the bed. She was asleep instantly. When she opened her eyes the next morning, she saw it was after ten o'clock. She dragged herself out of bed and stumbled into the kitchen, where Bertie sat quietly drinking a cup of coffee. The woman motioned her to help herself.

"Sleep okay?" the woman asked.

Roxie yawned. "I never turned over after I hit the pillow." She glanced around the kitchen as she spoke. It was bright and cheerful, painted in yellow. "I like your place," she said.

Bertie shrugged. "It's okay, I guess. Too big for one person, though. I keep thinking I should sell it and move into a one-bedroom condominium. But I wouldn't have room when my children and grandchildren visited." She sighed. "I raised my children in this house. It's filled with some special memories, you know?"

They talked a while longer, then Roxie returned to the bedroom, made the bed, and slipped into the dress she'd worn the night before. She combed her hair and brushed her teeth.

"Keep the toothbrush," Bertie said. "I can always go out and buy another. Something masculine, I think." They both laughed. Roxie hugged her, promised to visit once she found a new apartment, then hurried to her car. It was after lunchtime when she pulled into the driveway beside her apartment.

Roxie climbed out of her car and made her way

up the stairs to her apartment, holding her key ring in one hand. It looked as though it were going to be another hot day, she thought. She slipped the key into the lock and opened the door. She closed it behind her, then tossed her purse onto one chair. Out of the corner of her eye she caught movement in the shadows and fear rippled through her like a tidal wave. One hand flew to her heart, then she sighed her relief when she saw it was only Tyler. Tyler? What on earth was he doing there? she thought.

His face was a mask of anger, his eyes glowering. "Where the hell have you been?" he demanded without preamble. His long legs were stretched out on her couch as though he had every right to be there.

Roxie's gaze collided with his. For a moment she was stunned. How had he gotten into her apartment? Shock yielded instantly to fury. Her green eyes were hostile. "You're in *my* apartment," she said. "I ask the questions here." She was numb with rage. "For instance, what are you doing here!"

He gave her a thunderous look as he pulled himself up from the sofa. "Waiting," he said, contempt loud in his voice. "I've called the police department, the highway patrol, and every hospital within a fifty-mile radius."

Had the circumstances been different, Roxie might have felt sympathetic. He looked tired, and there were dark circles under his eyes. Instead she bristled with indignation. She was so furious, she could hardly put her thoughts together. "How dare you come into my apartment in my absence!" she finally cried out. "And how dare you question me as though I were a child. I don't owe you an explanation."

Tyler swallowed hard, trying to contain his anger. "I feel responsible for you." His words were clipped.

"Don't."

"I can't help it, dammit!"

"Then I'll move out immediately." She would sleep in the streets before she'd let the man run her life as her father had. She pivoted on her heel. He reached out and grasped her wrist, stopping her cold.

"I can't let you do that," he said, fear rushing in at the thought of her leaving.

"I can do what I please," she said, "and not you or anybody else is going to stop me."

"Roxie, I care for you. Can't you see that? I love you."

Her head snapped up, astonishment clear in her green eyes. "What?" Her voice rose in surprise. A delightful and unexpected warmth surged through her body.

"I love you," he repeated, stepping closer, his eyes filled with uncertainty. He had never felt more vulnerable in his life.

Tyler in love with her? She stared up at him for a moment before she raised one hand to his cheek. He caught her wrist and held it as though half afraid she might take it away. Then he turned his head slowly and pressed warm lips against her open palm.

"I love you too, Tyler," she whispered. He held open his arms, and she went to him willingly.

His body was hard and lean against hers. Roxie raised her lips to his, and he captured them. He kissed her deeply, urgently, and Roxie's stomach dipped as he ran his hands down her back and cupped one hip. He kneaded it gently, and a rush of heat spread through her belly.

Tyler's tongue swept through her mouth, seeking out every niche and tasting the sweetness. He reached behind her and pulled the white ribbon from her hair. Her thick mane fanned across her back. He tossed the ribbon aside and raked his fingers through her hair as he'd done a dozen times in his dreams, all the while kissing her. He moaned aloud as her tongue sought his, but he broke the kiss after a moment, to say, "Roxie, I don't think— "

"This isn't the time for thinking, Tyler," she whispered against his lips. "This is the time for feeling." As though trying to prove her point, she slid her hands beneath his cotton shirt and stroked the muscles of his chest. She would never have attempted something so bold with another man, but with Tyler it seemed natural. She had ached to run her hands over his chest many times, but nothing in her imagination had prepared her for the real thing. His muscles tensed at her touch, and she stroked them lovingly.

Tyler closed his eyes. He couldn't think straight.

He wanted her. He thought of her father briefly. "This is wrong," he said, his voice hoarse.

Roxie ran her lips up his throat and jaw. The tiny stubbles on his unshaven face felt wonderful against her skin. Now she realized why he had gone to such extremes to find her. "How can this be wrong if we love each other?" she asked.

Her face was glowing with love, and Tyler thought she had never looked more beautiful or tempting. Her fingers toyed with the curls on his chest, then teased his nipples, and a surge of desire shot through his loins. "You're a virgin," he said on a gasp.

"It doesn't matter."

How the hell was a man supposed to act in these circumstances? Her lips were everywhere, her hands coaxing his body in a way he couldn't help but respond to. "You're not prepared—"

She pulled back and looked into his eyes. "Yes I am," she said. "I took care of it a couple of weeks ago."

He knew then there was no turning back. He kissed her again and again, until their lips seemed to meld. Their breathing was hot and raspy. "Are you sure?" he said against her lips.

She nodded, knowing she had never been more sure of anything in her life. When Tyler suddenly swept her up in his arms and carried her toward the bedroom, she pressed her head against his chest. She could hear his heart beating. A feeling of apprehension stole over her. Wanting a man and actually making love with him were two different things entirely. What if she disappointed him?

Tyler could feel the blood pounding in his ears as he gently placed Roxie on the bed. She held her arms out and he went to her. Her passion-glazed eyes told him she wanted him. Still, he hesitated. "Roxie?"

"Love me, Tyler," she answered, slipping her arms around his neck. She pulled him close for another heated kiss. Her anxiety was alleviated as the kiss deepened, and she grew warm all over.

Tyler raised up and removed her shoes, taking a moment to caress her feet. His hands slid up her calves, past her knees to her thighs. Her silky pantyhose only heightened his desire, but he yearned to feel her naked flesh. Tyler moved cautiously, knowing he would have to be slow and gentle. As much as he desired her, this was no time to rush. He wanted the experience to be wonderful for her. Something she would remember always. Something she could treasure.

Roxie reached for the buttons on his shirt, and with trembling fingers managed to unbutton each one. His shirt fell open and exposed his wide chest. Roxie looked up and found him watching her closely. He was obviously leaving the decision with her. He would only take what she was prepared to offer. She dropped her gaze and plowed her fingers through his springy black chest hair and marveled at the masculine beauty before her.

Tyler leaned forward and kissed her. Suddenly his mouth was everywhere, her eyelids, the straight bridge of her nose. He nibbled his way to an ear-lobe, and his hot breath in her ear sent chills dancing along her spine.

Roxie vaguely was aware of him removing her pantyhose. Her wispy panties followed as he trailed hot kisses down her throat. He unfastened her dress and pulled it down her shoulders slowly, kissing each spot he bared.

When Roxie finally lay naked before him, he gazed at her, an expression of awed pleasure on his face. She was more beautiful than he'd imagined. She was the essence of femininity, and his heart swelled with pride because she loved him. He had known many beautiful women in his life, but none as lovely as this exquisite lady. He longed to look into her very soul, to know her as well as he knew himself.

Roxie wondered what Tyler was thinking. She had never revealed herself to a man before, and she was more than a little unsure of herself. The thought crossed her mind that he might not find her tempting, but his tender smile banished her worries.

"You're beautiful," he said, his voice almost reverent. Her small breasts were firm and tipped with coral nipples. He leaned forward and took one in his mouth. He felt her stiffen as he drew lazy circles around her nipple until it tightened. Once satisfied, he moved to the other breast, and teased it lovingly until she grasped his head and pulled him closer. Tyler moved with deliberate care. Although he was aroused beyond belief, gazing down at her soft curves and porcelain skin evoked soul-stirring emotions new to him.

Tyler's fingers trickled between the valley of her breasts, down her abdomen. She arched against his hand when his fingers delved into the patch of soft curls covering her femininity. She was warm and wet. Go slowly, he reminded himself. Take it slow.

Roxie crooned her pleasure as Tyler's fingers worked their magic between her thighs. His touch was light and gentle, creating wonderful new sensations. She wanted to return the pleasure, but she couldn't think straight. Her head spun in a wild kind of delirium.

When Tyler stood and peeled off his clothes, Roxie gazed at him in appreciation. He was magnificent, all and more than she'd ever dreamed he would be. Surely he would put an end to the sweet agony he had created inside her body. But as he lay naked beside her, he merely took her in his arms and kissed her as though purposely teasing her. One knee slipped between her thighs and pressed against the very crux of her desire. His hair-roughened skin chafed her sensitive inner thigh and fanned the heat within her. There seemed to be no end to it, and Roxie was certain she would lose her mind.

She whimpered his name, pleading with him to quench the fire that threatened to consume her. He swept her legs open and moved between them, the perspiration on his brow only hinting at how difficult it was for him to hold back. He probed her gently. "There will be pain."

"I don't care," she said, opening herself to him. She grasped his taut hips with her hands and held him, half afraid he might change his mind. The threat of pain didn't concern her in the least. What mattered most was ending the need.

Tyler entered her slowly and carefully, giving her body time to adjust to his fullness. His eyes probed hers for any sign of pain. There was none. He kissed her tenderly, knowing he loved her more than life itself. The realization hit him that this experience was as new to him as it was to her. He began moving against her and before long they moved in unison. Twice he slowed her, almost losing control when she grasped him so tightly. Surely she had been created just for him, he thought.

Roxie had never imagined that a man's body could feel so wonderful, could hold so many delights. Tyler filled her, and the friction of each carefully maneuvered thrust stoked the fires in her belly. She met each thrust, her nails digging into the taut muscles of his hips. Her head was spinning. Every inch of her body was sensitized to his slightest movement. Even her breasts knew the pleasure of his lovemaking as his chest hair chafed her nipples and made her breasts swell with desire.

Suddenly it all came together in a single mass of sensations and emotions. Each kiss, each powerful thrust, his scent—all seemed orchestrated for her pleasure. Her eyes searched his, and she found her own love mirrored in the fathomless depths. Her heart overflowed with love as sheer delight washed over her. Tears of love and release fell onto her cheeks, and Tyler collected them with his lips. She squeezed her eyes shut tightly as each wave intensified, and she bit her bottom lip to keep from crying out. Her body shivered as the last spasm receded. She heard Tyler call her name from far away, before he shuddered against her.

Several minutes later Tyler rolled off her, pulling her into his arms. Roxie snuggled beside him. He was damp with sweat. "Did I hurt you?" he asked gently.

"You could never hurt me."

"I love you," he whispered.

"I love you too," she said, feeling happy and groggy at the same time. He smelled nice, so wonderfully male. In his arms was where she belonged, she thought as she drifted off to sleep.

Nine

"I thought you knew how to cook," Tyler said, taking a bite of the bologna and cheese sandwich Roxie handed him.

She looked surprised. "What's wrong with this?" she said, eyeing her sandwich. "I live off this stuff."

He frowned. "This is all you eat?"

"Why should I buy a lot of groceries for one person?" She drained her glass of milk and stood. "Want more?" she asked, holding up her glass.

Tyler grinned. She looked delectable wearing his short-sleeve cotton shirt. It hung well past her bottom, but every time she leaned forward, he got a peek of her lacy panties. "Damn right I want more." He grabbed her around the waist and pulled her onto his lap. She squealed in protest, but they both knew it was halfhearted.

Roxie almost dropped her glass as she fell against

Tyler's naked chest. He wore only his jeans, and she couldn't keep her eyes off him. "You have a one-track mind, you know that?" She had awakened from her nap to find him anxious for more lovemaking. "What will Lela think? You've been over here all day."

"I could care less what Lela thinks. I'm a big boy."

"So I've noticed."

He grinned and reached for the buttons on his shirt and undid them with deft hands. When her breasts came into view, he gazed at them appreciatively before taking a rosy nipple between his lips. It tightened in response.

Roxie laid her head against his shoulder. The man's touch sent her into a fever. She felt less self-conscious with him now, and her own lips busied themselves at his ear. He shivered.

"Keep that up and you won't finish your sandwich."

"I'm not hungry anymore."

"Neither am I." He stood and swung her high into his arms. He paused and drew his brows together in concern. "Are you sore?"

"No, the hot bath helped." She remembered how pleasantly shocked she'd been when Tyler had barged into the bathroom and climbed in the tub with her. The man obviously didn't have a modest bone in his body, she realized. And he seemed determined to rid her of any demureness.

Tyler carried her back into the bedroom, where the tousled covers gave evidence of how they'd spent most of the day. Once again they fell onto the bed and tore at each other's clothing. He tugged at her wispy lace panties and in no time she lay before him in feminine splendor. For the first time in her life, Roxie Norris felt truly beautiful.

She knew she wasn't model material, but when Tyler stroked and kissed her and lost himself inside her, he made her feel as though she were the most gorgeous and desirable woman in the world. His passion knew no limits. As he laved her body with his moist tongue, she squirmed beneath him. When his tongue sought the pleasure point between her thighs, she was surprised but not disappointed. She had never known the many ways one could give pleasure, but she was determined to learn what pleased Tyler. Without hesitation she nibbled at his nipples and was delighted when they responded as her own had. She buried her face in the coarse hair, and it tickled her nose. His scent made her giddy. She inched her way across his hard stomach and circled his navel with her tongue. Tyler groaned and wound his fingers through her thick and lustrous hair.

Roxie saw the pleasure written in the lines of his handsome face, and she loved him more with each sigh of rapture that escaped his lips. She knew then why her parents had placed such emphasis on the love between a man and woman. She could not imagine sharing such intimacies with another man; she could not fathom wanting to taste and learn the textures of another man's body. He whispered her name, and she vowed in her heart she would love him forever.

When Roxie thought they had both been well satisfied, Tyler surprised her by arousing her once more. He entered her, and she was swept up in a wave of desire that was even more intense than ever before. She met his thrusts evenly. They found release together, and Tyler murmured words of love that bound them forever as one.

It was early evening when Tyler nudged Roxie awake on the couch in front of the portable television he'd carried over from the house. He chuckled. She'd nodded off several times. "C'mon, Red," he said, helping her up. "I think we both could use a little sleep." He hadn't slept much the night before and now he welcomed the chance to rest. Roxie let him guide her into the bedroom, and she climbed into bed, knowing she would drop off to sleep instantly. When she felt the mattress dip on the other side, she opened her eyes. "What will Lela think if you spend the night here?" she asked groggily.

"She'll think we made up," Tyler said, trying to arrange the covers on the bed.

She snuggled against him and sighed happily. "There goes my reputation."

Tyler frowned in the dark. He had never considered what anyone else would think, especially his hired hands. The last thing they needed to see was him slipping out of Roxie's apartment the next morning. He wouldn't spend the night and risk a bunch of tongues wagging behind her back.

He cared nothing of his own reputation, but he was determined not to see Roxie hurt.

Tyler was lying in the dark with his eyes open when the telephone jolted Roxie awake. She fumbled for it. "Hello?" she said, her brain fogged with sleep. Her green eyes widened when she realized it was her father on the other end. "Daddy?" She shot Tyler a frantic look.

Tyler sat upright in the bed as though a drill sergeant had just blasted reveille in one ear. "Oh, damn," he muttered under his breath.

"No, I'm not sick, Daddy," Roxie said. "I was just tired and decided to go to bed early." She stifled a yawn. "Yes, I have plenty of money, and no, I haven't changed my mind about coming home. I've already told you—" She glanced at Tyler and rolled her eyes as she listened to every argument her father had. Finally she sighed into the telephone. "I can't call you every day," she said, her voice taking on an assertive tone. "I can't afford it, and no, I don't want to call collect. Besides, I have my own life now." She listened to him for a moment. "I'm sorry if that hurts your feelings, but you're going to have to accept it. We've gone through this before. I'm not a child anymore; I'm twenty-five years old."

Roxie held the telephone away from her ear as her father continued to argue. "Daddy—" She tried to interrupt him. "Daddy, I'm not going to argue with you. As soon as I get settled in my new apartment, you can plan a visit."

Tyler's head snapped up. Settled in her new

apartment? She was planning to move after what had happened between them, for pete's sake?

"The car hasn't given me a bit of trouble," Roxie lied, crossing her fingers as she did so. "Now, good night, Daddy. Go to sleep and stop worrying about me."

Once Roxie hung up, she sighed heavily and covered her face with her hands. "Was I rude?" she asked Tyler, who dumbly shook his head. "Sometimes I have to be very blunt with my father in order to get through to him. He won't let go." She fitted herself into the crook of Tyler's arms once again. She yawned. She was too sleepy to think about her father and what she was going to do now that her relationship with Tyler had changed dramatically. She would think about it in the morning.

Tyler, on the other hand, was sure he wasn't going to get any sleep. He held Roxie in his arms as waves of guilt hit him.

When Roxie awoke the following morning, she was surprised to find Tyler's side of the bed empty. She yawned and stretched like a contented cat. She smiled, remembering how they'd spent the previous day, then climbed out of bed and went in search of him. But he was not in the apartment. He probably went home to shower and change, she thought.

Roxie showered and spent several minutes trying to choose something to wear. She took longer applying her makeup and doing her hair, knowing she wanted to look her best for Tyler. Once dressed, she hurried out of the apartment, down the stairs, and toward the house.

Lela looked up in surprise, when Roxie entered the kitchen. "Well, you don't *look* any different," the woman said, grinning. "I'll pour you a cup of coffee."

Roxie blushed to the roots of her hair. "I'm perfectly fine. Don't bother with the coffee, I made a cup of instant before I left the house. Where's Tyler?"

Lela didn't quite meet her gaze. "He's painting the barn."

"Painting the barn? What on earth for?"

"I reckon he's trying to work off his anger."

Roxie stared in disbelief. "He's angry?" She couldn't believe her ears. He certainly hadn't acted angry the day before. "Did he say *why* he was angry?"

"No, I was hoping you could answer that."

Roxie contemplated the situation for several minutes. Why had he slipped out during the night? Yesterday he had said he loved her. She had expected to wake up in his arms, but she'd awakened alone. Perhaps . . . Roxie shuddered at the possibility. She suddenly remembered some of the briefs her older sisters had passed on to her years before. Perhaps Tyler no longer respected her. Tears stung her eyes at the thought.

"What's wrong with you, honey?" Lela said, reaching for a tissue from a box on the counter and handing it to her. "You just tell ol' Lela what's ailing you and together we'll work it out."

"I'm so ashamed," Roxie said, tears streaming down her face. "After what happened yesterday—" She blushed, but Lela reached for her hand and squeezed it reassuringly. "He probably doesn't respect me anymore," Roxie said, choking on a sob. It sounded juvenile, but she couldn't imagine what other reason he could have for acting so strangely.

"That's the most ridiculous thing I've ever heard," Lela told her. "You gave him something precious, and you did it out of love. If you want my opinion, I think the man is running scared."

"From what?"

"From love, that's what." Lela's look softened. "Honey, Tyler ain't never had anybody who really loved him 'cept the man who raised him. And me, of course. From what little I know about his parents, they were no good and didn't care what happened to him. I guess that's why he shied away from relationships. Oh, he has had his share of women, but they never lasted long. It's different with you, though. He loves you. I can see it in his eyes." She folded her arms over her chest. "Why do you reckon he pitches such a fit every time one of the hired hands look at you?"

"What should I do?" Roxie asked, sniffing hard.

"Depends on how much you want him. I always say, if you want something bad enough you have to grab it."

"You're absolutely right, Lela," Roxie said. "What I did *was* done out of love. I expect love and commitment in return." She stalked toward the back door. "I'm not going to hide in my apartment in shame. I'm going to make him face up to the fact that he loves me."

"There you go," Lela said, cheering her on.

Roxie let herself out and marched toward the barn. She found Tyler scraping paint that had buckled and blistered after years of neglect. She did a double take at the sight of him in worn cutoffs, naked from the waist up.

"What are you doing?" Roxie asked.

Tyler jumped at the sound of her voice. "Dammit! Do you have to sneak up on people like that?"

"You're one to talk," she said, sarcasm lacing her voice. "You sneaked out of bed without saying good-bye."

"I didn't want to wake you," he said, trying not to look at her long legs beneath her cotton shorts.

"Obviously," she mumbled. She sensed he was angry, but had no idea what it could be about. "Why are you painting the barn?"

He returned his attention to his work. "Because it needs it."

"Lela said you were madder than a hornet. Any particular reason?"

Tyler picked up the shirt he'd had on before he'd gotten too hot. He had decided he needed to tackle a big project if he was going to try to get Roxie off his mind, and painting the barn had sounded like a good idea at the time. No doubt he could have picked cooler weather to do it. He mopped his forehead. "Look, Roxie, I'd rather not discuss it if you don't mind."

"Well, I do mind," she snapped. "Yesterday you

said you loved me. You couldn't keep your hands off me. Today you're back to your old games. I'm tired of it, Tyler. You either love me or you don't."

Tyler was struggling. It was written all over his face. "It's not that simple, Roxie."

"As far as I'm concerned it is."

"It just wouldn't work between us."

"Why, Tyler? Why wouldn't it work?" Roxie was beginning to worry now. Something was standing between them. She could feel it. But she had no idea what it was.

"Because," he said. "Just because."

Roxie's temper flared. She balled her hands into fists by her side. "That's a lousy excuse and you know it."

Tyler raked one hand through his hair. "Roxie, there are things you don't know about—"

Roxie covered her ears with her hands. "I don't want to know about your past, Tyler. I love you for who you are now. I'm only concerned about the future."

"You don't understand." He couldn't have a relationship with her, not after he had deceived her for so long. Guilt ate at his gut.

"I understand perfectly, mister love-em-and-leave-em. And if you think for one minute I'm going to let you turn your back on me after what happened between us yesterday, you're full of baloney." She reached for one of several paint brushes he'd tossed in a pile.

"What are you doing?" he asked.

"I'm going to help you paint the barn," she said matter-of-factly.

"Oh, for heaven's sake," he muttered. It was bad enough that he couldn't get the woman out of his mind. Why did she insist on driving him crazy in person? "We can't paint the barn right now," he said. "It has to be scraped, possibly sanded, primed, then painted."

"Forgive me," she said haughtily. "I thought we were painting an old barn, not a Rembrandt."

"I didn't ask for your help," he said. "Besides, I thought you had to go to the university and look for an apartment."

Roxie's heart turned over in her chest. Looking for another apartment was the last thing she wanted to do at the moment. After spending the previous day in his arms and listening to his confessions of love, she'd decided to put her plans on hold for a couple of days. One way or the other, she was determined to find out exactly where she stood with Tyler Sheridan.

Three days later, Roxie and Tyler had scraped the entire barn and had started applying the first coat of paint. Roxie, who hated to paint anything larger than her fingernails, had used up her patience at the job on her apartment. Now, she merely wanted to slop the paint on and be done with it. But Tyler, apparently a perfectionist, insisted it had to be smoothed on just so. Their arguments, Lela said, could be heard clear to the next county.

The August temperatures had climbed, making

outside work unbearable, but Tyler persisted, even though he told Roxie to go inside several times. But she wouldn't give up. Because her fair skin had become badly sunburned under the grueling rays, Roxie had donned a baggy long-sleeved shirt. Her shoulders felt raw beneath the starched cotton fabric. She had spent the previous night tossing and turning in her bed with chills, chafing her flesh on the sheets. She had gone into the bathroom upon waking that morning and found her eyes puffy and her skin blotched.

Tyler had been perched on a ladder all morning, forcing himself to ignore Roxie as he had since they'd begun the project. She was hell-bent on getting his attention. She'd worn her cutoff shorts with only a halter the past few days, but he was determined to keep his eyes on his work and not her. Today, he noticed briefly, she had put on jeans and a baggy shirt and hadn't tried to start a conversation with him. She worked quietly on the bottom section. Perhaps it was because she was unusually quiet that he looked down from the ladder. He frowned and climbed down.

"Are you okay?" Tyler asked, watching her slather the paint on the board just as he had taught her.

"I'm fine."

When she didn't look up, Tyler stooped and peered at her. "What in the hell happened to your face?"

Roxie was too tired and miserable to look up. "I have a sunburn."

"You have a helluva lot more than a sunburn,"

he said. "Here, let me help you up." She didn't offer a hand, so he reached beneath both her arms and pulled her up. Her face and throat were a nasty shade of red. Roxie watched him unbutton a couple of the buttons on her shirt, but she felt too ill to object.

"Good grief, Roxie," he said. "You've got sun poisoning. Why didn't you tell me?" Before she had a chance to answer, he turned her in the direction of her apartment. "I want you to go run a cool bath," he said, already prodding her to move. "Fill the tub as full as you can and get in. I'm going to see what Lela has for burns."

Roxie nodded weakly and made her way toward the stairs leading up to her apartment. Her flesh felt tight and hot. The stairs loomed over her like a mountain, and she climbed them slowly. Once inside, she headed straight for the bathroom and turned on the water, making sure it was cool. She winced as she peeled her clothes off. Tiny blisters spotted her shoulders. She stepped into the tub and inched herself into the water. It felt like ice water against her feverish flesh. After a moment she immersed her entire body.

When Tyler entered the bathroom several minutes later, he found Roxie shivering in the bathtub. "Lela gave me something for your burn," he said, shaking his head when he saw how bad she looked. "You're going to have to sit in the water for at least twenty minutes to cool off." He stooped beside the tub, grabbed a washcloth, and wet it.

He squeezed it and let the water trickle down her back.

"Why didn't you tell me how sensitive your skin is?" he asked. "You have no business working out in that sun." Lord, he felt like a jerk.

Roxie was too tired to argue. He would have noticed how burned she was had he not been so intent on ignoring her the past couple of days. "It . . . d-doesn't m-matter," she said, shivering. But she realized how ridiculous she'd been, wearing shorts and halters in the heat of the day, knowing how sensitive her fair skin was.

Once Roxie had sat in the water long enough, Tyler helped her out and patted her dry with a towel. "Go lie on the bed," he said. "I'll be in there in a second."

Roxie nodded dumbly and wrapped the towel around her, knotting it securely over one breast. When Tyler returned, he was carrying a small washbasin and a roll of paper towels. "What is that?" she asked weakly.

"Witch hazel. Lela told me how to make compresses." He set the basin by the bed. "You're going to have to get rid of the towel, Roxie, and turn over on your stomach."

Roxie shot him a dirty look before she turned over on the bed. She pulled the towel down to her waist, baring her back and shoulders. She heard Tyler tear off paper towels and wet them in the basin. Next he placed the wet towels on her shoulders, and she sighed her relief. "That feels good," she said.

"It'll take away the burn," he said. "Then I'll rub this salve on you." Once Tyler felt he had taken care of her back, he helped her turn over so he could get the front. Although she tried to cover her breasts, he still got a peek and couldn't help but smile. He placed compresses above her breasts, across her stomach and thighs. He laughed. "I can't wait till you start peeling," he said.

She rolled her eyes. "I'm going to have more freckles."

"I love freckles."

"So I've noticed," she said, unable to keep the sarcasm out of her voice.

Tyler felt his guilt resurface. He really had been a brute the past couple of days. He had wanted to tell her a hundred times what he was feeling. He wasn't trying to push her away, he was trying to get rid of the guilt. He knew it was time he made a few decisions. "We need to talk, Roxie," he said. "Not right now. First I want you to rest, then we'll talk. Do you have any aspirin?"

"Bathroom cabinet." Roxie sighed when he left the room. Perhaps he was ready to air the problems between them, she thought. She was prepared to wait, though. Right now she was in no condition to have a serious conversation.

Tyler returned with aspirin tablets and water. He raised Roxie's head slightly so she could swallow them. Once the compresses had dried, he rubbed the salve into her flesh as gently as he could, and, when he'd covered her with it, he stripped the top covers off the bed. The towel covered part of her body. "Think you can rest now?" he asked.

She closed her eyes and nodded, thankful that her skin had cooled somewhat.

Tyler stood in the doorway for a long time, gazing down at her as she slept. All he had ever wanted to do was look after her as her father had asked. At least until she was settled in.

He had never counted on falling deeply in love with her. As a result, he had hurt her more times than he cared to acknowledge. He felt like a first-rate bastard. He had played both sides of the fence, so to speak, and Roxie had suffered the consequences.

Ten

Tyler woke Roxie several times during the night to drink a glass of juice. "You don't want to risk dehydration," he said. She awoke sometime later, moaning, and Tyler was instantly at her side. Once again he made compresses, and rubbed salve gently into her parched skin. He gave her a glass of lemonade to wash down two more aspirin. Once he helped her to the bathroom, then back to the bed where she spent the rest of the night, tossing restlessly. The sheets felt like sandpaper against her flesh, and every time she moved, her shoulders ached and burned. At one point she dreamed Lela had come into the room to check on her. It was dawn before the pain subsided enough so she could sleep comfortably.

When Roxie opened her eyes again, sunlight filled the room. She glanced up and saw Lela standing over her. "How do you feel, honey?" the woman asked, placing one plump hand against Roxie's forehead.

"Better, I think," Roxie said. Her skin was still tight and hot, but she didn't feel as though she were on fire.

"I brought you a breakfast tray. Nothing fancy, just some sliced strawberries and melon. It's in the fridge when you want it."

Roxie nodded. "I dreamed you stopped by last night."

Lela smiled. "That wasn't a dream. I came over a couple of times to check on you. You were hot as a firecracker."

"Where's Tyler?"

"Asleep on the couch." Lela grinned. "I think he paced the floor most of the night. Serves him right if you ask me, after the way he's been acting the last couple of days." She glanced at her wrist-watch. "Well, I best get back to the house. Clem will be knocking on the back door any minute wanting to get in. You need anything?" When Roxie shook her head, Lela nodded. "I'll stop by this afternoon to check on you."

"I'll be fine," Roxie assured her.

When Tyler woke, Roxie was dressed and in the kitchen eating some of the fruit Lela had dropped off. "How are you feeling this morning?" he asked.

She smiled weakly. "I think I'll live, thanks to you. I understand you didn't get much sleep last night." He shrugged. "Want a cup of instant cof-fee?" she asked. When he made a move for the stove, she stopped him. "You've done enough," she insisted, noticing the tired look on his face.

Tyler took a seat at the table. "You're going to need to take it easy for the next couple of days," he said. He thanked her when she finally set a cup of coffee before him. He took a slow, tentative sip. When he glanced up, she was sitting across from him at the table watching him expectantly. "What's wrong?"

Roxie folded her hands in her lap and looked at them. "You said we were going to have a talk once I felt better."

Tyler sighed audibly. He had known in his heart the day would come when he'd have to level with Roxie if he expected to have a relationship with her. He couldn't go on deceiving her. A relationship had to be based on love and honesty, and he owed it to her if he expected the same in return.

But gazing at her over the rim of his coffee cup convinced him it wasn't going to be easy. He had rehearsed his speech several times during the night as he watched her sleep, but now he couldn't grasp one single sentence. "I owe you an apology," he finally said. "Not only you, but your father as well. I've deceived you both."

Roxie's face went blank. "Why on earth would you owe my father an apology?" she asked. "And what do you mean you've deceived us? In what way?"

He took a deep breath. He had put it off as long as he could. It was now or never. "Roxie, your father wrote to me several weeks before you came to Charleston. He asked me to offer you a job at the Southern Belle." He hesitated. 'He also asked me to keep an eye on you. Before you had your telephone installed he called me frequently to check on you."

Roxie froze. Her heart pounded wildly in her chest. She couldn't believe what she'd just heard. "Why are you telling me this?"

Tyler leaned forward on both elbows. "Because I love you, Roxie, and I feel like a jerk. I never wanted to be the middleman, but I owed your father."

"So you were trying to repay an old favor by being nice to me," she said simply, feeling a raw ache in the pit of her stomach.

"In the beginning, yes. But all that changed once I met you."

Roxie laughed out loud, but her eyes stung with unshed tears. "Well, you both fooled me," she said. "I never suspected a thing. I was so proud of myself. I thought, gee, here I had all these problems in the beginning. But in the end, I overcame them and got a job and an apartment in no time." She laughed again, and this time a single tear slid down her cheek. She swiped at it angrily. "But it was all *planned*, wasn't it?" she said, standing. "And I played right into your hands."

"I never planned to fall in love with you, Roxie." Tyler stood and reached for her, but she backed away.

"You're no different from the man who raised me," she said. "In fact, you're worse. At least I knew where I stood with my father, but you underhandedly tried to run my life."

"Roxie, let me explain—"

"You've already explained," she said coolly, "and I don't want to hear anything else."

"But I love you."

"That isn't a cure-all, Tyler." She turned on her heel and left the room.

Tyler followed. "Roxie, would you listen to me," he said as he watched her pull a suitcase from beneath her bed. "What are you doing?"

"That should be obvious." She opened it, then pulled out several drawers from the dresser. She dumped the contents into the suitcase. She saw the dumbfounded look on Tyler's face and ignored it.

"Where are you going?" he finally asked.

"I haven't the slightest idea," she said simply.

"But you said you loved me."

"That was before I knew you were in cahoots with my father. I'm not going to trade my father for someone as bad." She hurried into the bathroom and grabbed her makeup and dumped it into a pouch, then tossed it into the suitcase with the rest of her belongings. She scooped up her shoes and dumped them in as well, before closing her suitcase and snapping the locks.

"I can't let you walk out of my life," Tyler said, suddenly terrified at the thought of losing her.

She gave him a smug look. "Just watch me." She picked up the suitcase and hurried out of the room, grabbing her purse as she went. She was sure there were a lot of things she'd left behind, but she would worry about that later. Right now all she wanted to do was get away from Tyler as fast as she could. She couldn't think straight when he was around.

She opened the screen door and let it slam in Tyler's face as she cleared the stairs at record-breaking speed. Tyler followed. She opened the door of her car and shoved her suitcase in the back seat. She climbed in. Tyler held the door and refused to let her close it.

"You're making a big mistake, Roxie," he said, his own temper rising. "You're angry. Why don't you stop and think before you walk out on me?"

"I'm not angry, Tyler," she said calmly. "I'm embarrassed and hurt. Humiliated. And I really don't want to look you in the face right now. I gave you everything I had. I shared something . . . something sacred with you. And you made a complete fool out of me. You and my father."

"What was I supposed to do, refuse your father the favor? The man kept me out of prison. He cared enough to take me into his own home until he could find a place for me to live. Nobody else would have done that for me, Roxie." When he saw she wasn't listening, he almost yelled. "Are you just going to walk away from the fact that I love you?" he asked.

"I'm not sure what I'm going to do. But whatever I decide, I'll have the satisfaction of knowing it's my decision." She slammed the door and locked it, then grabbed the keys from her purse. She put one of the keys into the ignition and turned it. Her car roared to life. Tyler banged on the window, but she refused to look at him. She was near tears again. She needed space. She stepped on the gas and her tires spit gravel as the car squealed away.

"You can't turn your back on what we have," Tyler shouted. But it was useless. She was already gone. He glanced at the house and saw Lela standing at the back door. She shook her head and disappeared inside.

"If you've come here looking for a good time, forget it," the tall angular woman said, giving Roxie a stern look. "This is the YWCA. We have a reputation to uphold."

"Believe me, Miss Bix," Roxie said, "I took one look at this place and knew I wasn't going to have a good time." She counted out several bills into the woman's open palm.

"There'll be no drinking or men on the premises," the woman continued as though reading from a book. "If I discover either, you will be evicted without a refund. Is that clear?"

Roxie picked up her suitcase. "Perfectly. Would you please show me to my room?"

The woman opened the drawer of her desk, stuck the money inside, and locked the drawer before escorting Roxie down a gloomy hall. She passed several rooms before coming to a halt at a door near the end of the hall. "There are a lot of elderly women staying here," she said, unlocking the door. "If you have a radio or television, I would appreciate your keeping it turned low after ten o'clock." She pushed the door open.

Roxie stepped inside a small, sparsely furnished room. The woman came in beside her. "You'll have to share a bathroom with several other people. It's the third door down the hall on your right. You'll get fresh towels daily, and I change the sheets every Friday. Any questions?"

"I think you've covered everything," Roxie said, thankful she had paid for only three nights. She'd at least have time to sort things out and look for an apartment. After thanking the woman, she closed the door and locked it, placed her suitcase beside a scratched dresser, and sat on the bed. She was exhausted. She had driven around for hours before deciding to come to the YWCA. She knew she looked strange wearing only her romper and a tear-stained face. Perhaps that's why Miss Bix had gone over the rules so carefully.

Roxie was sure she had cried enough tears to last a lifetime. She knew deep in her heart that she loved Tyler. But the fact that he had been able to kiss her and make love to her, while withholding the truth about his relationship with her father, hurt terribly, although she understood now why he had backed off several times. But why hadn't he told her the truth? Was his sense of obligation to her father stronger than his love for her? Obviously it was.

Roxie lay back on the bed and stared at the

ceiling for a long time. Her eyes felt puffy, and her sunburn hurt. She hadn't thought to bring the salve with her. Her stomach growled and reminded her she hadn't eaten anything other than the fruit she'd had that morning. She closed her eyes. Perhaps after she rested she would drive to a pharmacy and buy something to rub on her burned shoulders. Then she'd pick up a sandwich. Yes, after she rested. Things were bound to seem better then.

Roxie was jolted awake sometime later by a noise in the hall. The room was dim. She glanced at her wristwatch and saw she had slept for most of the day. It was after six o'clock. The commotion outside continued. A woman yelled. Someone was banging on a door. She heard a man's voice.

Tyler's voice.

Roxie's jaw dropped open. How had he found her? She felt her pulse race as the banging grew closer. She heard Miss Bix's threatening voice. Roxie jumped when Tyler banged on her door. She stood, not knowing what to do. Tyler was yelling for her to open up. Miss Bix sounded hysterical.

Damn the man! What right did he have to hunt her down when she had made it clear she didn't want to see him? Not only that, he was embarrassing her, she thought, her temper flaring. Roxie marched to the door, flipped open the locks, and jerked it open. Tyler appeared both surprised and relieved to see her.

"What are you doing here?" Roxie demanded, planting her hands on her hips. She was further embarrassed to see several elderly ladies peeking out from behind their doors. Miss Bix stood only a few feet away, looking as though she wanted to wring Tyler's neck.

"I have searched all over town for you," he said. "I finally called the police and they located your car."

"So? You found me. Now go away." She started to close the door, but he blocked it with his foot. "Leave me alone, Tyler," she said, gritting her teeth.

Miss Bix came closer. "Mister, you have five seconds to leave before I have you arrested."

Tyler waved the threat aside. "I'm not leaving without her," he said, motioning to Roxie.

"Go ahead and call the police," Roxie told the landlady. "It'll do him good to spend a couple of nights in jail."

Tyler looked hurt. "I can't believe you said that."

"And I can't believe you send the authorities out looking for me every time I leave my apartment." As she spoke, Miss Bix stalked off in a huff.

"Roxie, would you give me a chance to tell you how I feel?" he asked, his foot still stuck between the door and the frame. "You have every right to be angry. I realize now how important it was for you to be on your own. And you were on your own. You're the one who asked for a job at the

Southern Belle, you didn't wait for me to offer you the job. You're the one who worked so hard. You cared enough to make changes to benefit the waitresses. And I would never have come up with the idea of your moving into that apartment. You're the one who went to the trouble of painting it and fixing it up, even when I offered to pay someone to do it. Anybody else would have balked at the idea of staying there."

Roxie wasn't going to give in. "Okay, Tyler, you've had your say. Now would you go?"

"I love you, Roxie," he said, trying to meet her dark gaze through the crack in the door. "I started falling in love with you the day you had that fit in front of my restaurant." When she didn't answer, he persisted. "Do you think I would have kept you on as a waitress at the Southern Belle if I hadn't loved you?"

"I wasn't *that* bad," she muttered.

"You were worse than bad," he said. "Not only are you a terrible waitress, but you have one hell of a stubborn streak running through you. Your father agreed with me on that score."

Roxie frowned. "My father? When did you speak with my father?"

"After you left this morning. I told him I'd fallen in love with you and wanted to marry you. He said yes. Not right away, mind you. It took me a good hour to get him used to the idea. In the end he said it was your decision."

Tyler wanted to marry her?

"So what do you say, Red? Will you marry me?"

Roxie literally was stunned by his marriage proposal. Her grip loosened on the doorknob, and Tyler used it to his advantage, shoving the door open. Roxie threw herself into his arms.

"Does this mean yes?" he asked hopefully.

Her face, which had been drawn in grief before, was now radiant. "Only if you promise not to have me followed every time I leave the house. And we'll make decisions together. Fifty-fifty."

Tyler kissed her on the tip of her nose. "I don't want to run your life, Roxie. I just want to love you. As far as your father is concerned, I think he has decided to let go. But I felt I owed it to him to bring things out in the open." He grinned at her shocked expression. "Not *everything*, he added.

Five minutes later they hurried out the door of the YWCA, Tyler carrying Roxie's suitcase. "What about the job opening at the Southern Belle?" she said.

Tyler shrugged. "What about it?"

"Is the offer still open? I love working with you."

He smiled. "I think we can work something out."

Roxie followed him to his car and he opened the door. "What about my car?" she asked. "I can't leave it here."

Tyler rolled his eyes. "I guarantee you nobody is going to steal it, Red. They probably wouldn't even be able to get the damn thing started." When she shot him a dirty look, he laughed. "I think I've figured out what to buy you for a wedding present." He opened the door and set her suitcase in the back. Once he'd climbed in beside her, he surprised her by taking her in his arms.

"I don't ever want you to run away from me again, Red." His lips captured hers in a heated kiss. When he finally ended the kiss, he noticed a flashing light behind them. He glanced around and saw a patrol car with its blue light spinning.

"Damn," Tyler muttered. "That old bag really did call the police." He shot Roxie a skeptical look. "Think maybe your father could get me out of this one?"

"Sorry," she said, trying to swallow her laughter. "You're on your own this time."

Tyler climbed out of the car. "Don't start the honeymoon without me," he said before closing the door.

Roxie laughed as she watched him make his way toward a frowning policeman. She couldn't think of a better way to spend her life than married to Tyler Sheridan.

THE EDITOR'S CORNER

Bantam Books has a *very* special treat for you next month—Nora Roberts's most ambitious, most sizzling novel yet . . .

SWEET REVENGE

Heroine Adrianne, the daughter of a fabled Hollywood beauty and an equally fabled Arab playboy, leads a remarkable double life. The paparazzi and the gossip columnists know her as a modern princess, a frivolous socialite flitting from exclusive watering spot to glittering charity ball. No one knows her as The Shadow, the most extraordinary jewel thief of the decade. She hones her skills at larceny as she parties with the superrich, stealing their trinkets and baubles just for practice . . . for she has a secret plan for the ultimate heist—a spectacular plan to even a bitter score. Her secret is her own until Philip Chamberlain enters her life. Once a renowned thief himself, he's now one of Interpol's smartest, toughest cops . . . and he's falling wildly in love with Adrianne!

SWEET REVENGE will be on sale during the beginning of December when your LOVESWEPTs come into the stores. Be sure to ask your bookseller right now to reserve a copy especially for you.

Now to the delectable LOVESWEPTs you can count on to add to your holiday fun . . . and excitement.

Our first love story next month carries a wonderful round number—LOVESWEPT #300! **LONG TIME COMING,** by Sandra Brown, is as thrilling and original as any romance Sandra has ever written. Law Kincaid, the heart-stoppingly handsome astronaut hero, is in a towering rage when he comes storming up Marnie Hibbs's front walk. He thinks she has been sending him blackmail letters claiming he has a teenage son. As aghast as she is, and still wildly attracted to Law, whom she met seventeen years before when she was just a teen, Marnie tries to put him off and hold her secret close. But the golden and glorious man is determined to wrest the truth from her at any cost! A beautiful love story!

(continued)

Welcome back Peggy Webb, author of LOVESWEPT #301, **HALLIE'S DESTINY,** a marvelous love story featuring a gorgeous "gypsy" whom you met in previous books, Hallie Donovan. A rodeo queen with a heart as big as Texas, Hallie was the woman Josh Butler wanted—he knew it the second he set eyes on her! Josh was well aware of the havoc a bewitching woman like Hallie could wreak in a man's life, but he couldn't resist her. When Josh raked her with his sexy golden eyes and took her captive on a carpet of flowers, Hallie felt a miraculous joy . . . and a great fear, for Josh couldn't—wouldn't—share his life and its problems with her. He sets limits on their love that drive Hallie away . . . until neither can endure without the other. A thrilling romance!

New author Gail Douglas scores another winner with **FLIRTING WITH DANGER,** LOVESWEPT #302. Cassie Walters is a spunky and gorgeous lady who falls under the spell of Bret Parker, a self-made man who is as rich as he is sexy . . . and utterly relentless when it comes to pursuing Cassie. Bret's not quite the womanizer the press made him out to be, as Cassie quickly learns. (I think you'll relish as much as I did the scene in which Michael and Cassie see each other for the first time. Never has an author done more for baby powder and diapers than Gail does in that encounter!) Cassie is terrified of putting down roots . . . and Bret is quite a family man. He has to prove to the woman with whom he's fallen crazily in love that she is brave enough to share his life. A real charmer of a love story crackling with excitement!

In **MANHUNT,** LOVESWEPT #303, Janet Evanovich has created two delightfully adorable and lusty protagonists in a setting that is fascinating. Alexandra Scott—fed up with her yuppie life-style and yearning for a husband and family—has chucked it all and moved to the Alaskan wilderness. She hasn't chosen her new home in a casual way; she's done it using statistics—in Alaska men outnumber women four to one. And right off the bat she meets a man who's one in a million, a dizzyingly attractive avowed bachelor, Michael Casey. But Alex can't be rational about Michael; she loses her head, right along with her heart to him. And to capture him she has to be shameless in her seduction. . . . A true delight!

Get ready to be transported into the heart of a small Southern town and have your funny bone tickled while your

(continued)

heart is warmed when you read **RUMOR HAS IT,** LOVE-SWEPT #304, by Tami Hoag. The outrageous gossip that spreads about Nick Leone when he comes to town to open a restaurant has Katie Quaid as curious as every other woman in the vicinity. She's known as an ice princess, but the moment she and Nick get together she's melting for him. You may shed a tear for Katie—she's had unbearable tragedy in her young life—and you'll certainly gasp with her when Nick presents her with a shocking surprise. A wonderfully fresh and emotionally moving love story!

That marvelous Nick Capoletti you met in Joan Elliott Pickart's last two romances gets his own true love in **SERENITY COVE,** LOVESWEPT #305. When Pippa Pauling discovered Nick Capoletti asleep on the floor of the cabin he'd rented in her cozy mountain lake resort, she felt light-headed with longing and tempted beyond resistance. From the second they first touched, Nick knew Pippa was hearth and home and everything he wanted in life. But Pippa feared that the magic they wove was fleeting. No one could fall in love so fast and make it real for a lifetime. But leave it to Capoletti! In a thrilling climax that takes Pippa and Nick back to Miracles Casino in Las Vegas and the gang there, Pippa learns she can indeed find forever in Nick's arms. A scorching and touching romance from our own Joan Elliott Pickart!

Also in Bantam's general list next month is a marvelous mainstream book that features love, murder, and shocking secrets—**MIDNIGHT SINS,** by new author Ellin Hall. This is a fast-paced and thrilling book with an unforgettable heroine. Don't miss it.

Have a wonderful holiday season.

Carolyn Nichols

Carolyn Nichols
Editor
LOVESWEPT
Bantam Books
666 Fifth Avenue
New York, NY 10103